The Hellbound
Detective

F.R. Jameson

To V and E, with love, always.

All Ghostly Shadows tales can be read as stand-alone,
but they all take place in the same universe.
Sort of

Also by F.R. Jameson in paperback

Ghostly Shadows
Death at the Seaside
Certain Danger
Won't You Come Save Me
Call of the Mandrake

Screen Siren Noir
Diana Christmas
Eden St. Michel
Alice Rackham

CHAPTER ONE

"So, are you the faithful retainer?" she asked.

It's hard for me to truly know, as sometimes even the most skilled Nevada poker player can be caught off guard, but I hoped my face didn't give away every ounce of contempt with which the question filled me. I hoped the bland mask I now constantly wore fixed itself into nothing more than mild distaste.

The woman who sat before me, in one of the ugliest coats it had ever been my misfortune to lay eyes on, was a journalist.

A note had come to my room earlier that afternoon informing me of a phone call at the front desk. On a crackling line, which gave the aural impression of being transatlantic (but surely wasn't), I was told of this irritatingly, nosey woman who was looking into the affairs of my employer, Jacob Ravens. The last few days, apparently, she had asked endless questions about him. Clearly she was someone who had never been warned of the danger of playing with white flame.

The instruction passed to me, through this intermediary whom I had never met, was to deal with her.

She had already been provided with my name, I was told, and was no doubt on her way to me right then.

As such the best strategy for me was to stay in plain sight and, sure enough, while I sat in the corner of the hotel's public bar that evening trying to warm myself with a large glass of rum, she approached me.

"Excuse me, are you Algernon Swafford?"

I glared at her. It didn't stop her smiling as ingratiatingly as her round and yet pinched in the middle face would allow. Without waiting for so much as a nodded invite, she took the seat in front of me.

In an instant, I had judged her. This woman was an unpleasant ball of curiosity and impertinence.

Appearance-wise, she was as wide as she was tall and the sky blue, heavy woollen coat she wore made her resemble a perfect square which had grown itself a pair of chunky legs. The coat was a particularly disgusting garment, one which was at bursting point around her ample bosom. I would have assumed she'd borrowed it from a slimmer friend, if it didn't match exactly the woollen hat perched on top of her head.

Every man, when faced with an antagonist of the fairer sex, would prefer them to be young and pretty. To give the eyes something pleasant to gaze at. But what really annoyed me about her wasn't her appearance, it was her assumptions. She *assumed* she could bother me, she *assumed* I was going to speak to her, she *assumed* I would be won over by her charms — no matter how well hidden they were.

Without waiting for my permission, she had sat, removed her spiral notepad from her bag and was gazing expectantly at me. Operating on the damned presumption I had a duty to answer her questions.

People say American women have become less

docile since The War, but at least they remember their damn manners.

"I'm Molly Wise, by the way. I imagine – from one of your colleagues – you've heard of me." She extended her hand and I gave it the most cursory of shakes. "Algernon Swafford? It's not a particularly American name, is it?"

"I'm not an American," I snarled as politely as possible.

"Oh right. Now you speak, I can of course tell from your accent." She bent her head and scribbled a few indistinct shorthand symbols. She was a Scot and I have always had a deep distaste for the Scots – particularly those Scottish women with an endless perkiness in their voices. "But I understood you are based primarily in California?"

I nodded. California based, but having to cope with the deepest gloom of an English winter. Such was the way my luck had turned.

"When did you move from here to there?" she asked.

"I sailed in Nineteen Twenty-Two."

"To do what?"

"Well, eventually I became a private investigator."

"A detective?" Her blue-grey eyes widened; they were her only redeeming feature. This surprise was artifice, no doubt. I'm sure she'd already discovered a great deal about me. "Like Humphrey Bogart?"

"Mr Bogart isn't a detective, he's a Hollywood actor, Miss Wise."

I'd met Bogart once. I was hired by the third Mrs Bogart to determine if he really was having a dalliance with the young girl who became the fourth Mrs Bogart. Of course he was and my photos were used to make sure she got a healthy divorce settlement.

The practice I'd built for myself in Los Angeles operated at the upper echelons of society. I had a certain kind of client. Anyone who didn't have a number of zeroes after their name, or a distinct type of breeding, would have been hurled out of my office before even being offered a glass of water. I was careful as to who I chose to represent and I had every reason to be. An extra service I offered, known to those who were very much the cream of the cream, was that I could not only find a problematic person, I could make sure they never bothered anyone again. Obviously this wasn't a service I could put on my business cards, not without attracting the sweaty attentions of the LAPD, but it meant I had to keep my client list at the more exclusive end of the Hollywood world.

In dark, wintery London though, my life as a proper Los Angeles detective seemed aeons ago.

The public bar where we sat had actually thrown cash at a most spectacular Christmas tree. It dominated a whole corner. So large it really didn't suit the room at all. However, every one of the decorations was flimsy paper and really could have been made by a small child with a pair of safety scissors. The tree was lovely, but as it was Boxing Day, the glow had come off it. It had started wilting to meet the level of its decorations, it looked tarnished – much as this whole stupid country was.

"So, are you still a detective?" she asked.

I took a sip of my rum. It made my oesophagus seem a fraction warmer, but the effect dissipated by the time it reached my gut.

"Yes, I am after a fashion," I murmured.

Another singsong had burst loud the other side of

the bar. There wasn't a piano (thank the Lord), but two couples were attempting to compensate for its absence by singing patriotic songs at the top of their voices. I thought maybe my answer would be drowned out by 'It's a Long Way to Tipperary', but the Scot's hearing was too keen.

"What do you mean?" she asked.

"I mean I have an exclusive relationship with one particular client."

"And this client is Jacob Ravens, isn't it?"

I neither confirmed, nor denied it.

The woman flicked to an earlier page in her notebook. It was all for damn show, of course. She didn't need to be reminded who she was looking into.

"Jacob Ravens. British horror author. His place of birth isn't clear, nor is much of his past, but he has made a name and a small fortune writing weird and disturbing tales in those 'pulp' magazines which I understand are so popular in your adopted country. A big enough name has he built for himself, Jonathan Cape has actually released a collected works in hardback in the UK. I understand it has sold very well. Enough for Ravens to support his younger wife and all the mistresses he seems to have. As well as – it transpires – his own private detective. So, are you the faithful retainer?"

I ignored her question and she pressed on:

"However, it might surprise you to know that despite my sex, I am not a reporter interested in showbiz tittle-tattle. No, I leave all the trivial nonsense to young Mr Cheesewright because it suits his proclivities more and besides, he guards his patch like a vicious dog.

"No, I am a crime reporter. And Ravens's name has

emerged, has been mentioned more than once in fact, in a case I am currently investigating. I am looking into the disappearance of a Cressida Monroe. The daughter of a vicar in the Midlands who was a natural beauty and had a lot of suitors. One of the more persistent, apparently, was your exclusive client, Jacob Ravens."

Cressida Monroe? I had never heard of her. However, knowing Ravens's nature, nothing would surprise me.

It was 1949 and there was less than a week left of this bloody decade. And because I found myself in an exclusive relationship with this demon of a man, and was therefore no longer in a position to refuse the work, I had been sent across to this miserable and damp land of my birth for some unspecified reason. I had two rooms on the second floor of The Addlestone Hotel in Marylebone. My initial impression of the place was that it was a poky little dive, but – having reacquainted myself with the rest of the city – I was starting to think that Ravens had actually spent cash on me. It wasn't one of the fanciest places, true, but a sink and running water in the room – as well as a toilet on the same floor – seemed like Beverly Hills luxury compared to some of the hovels offering accommodation I'd walked past.

Everything was smaller here; everything and everyone was faded and tired.

I'd been here three weeks and I had thought it might give me a chance to get out from under Ravens's thumb, but of course he was always with me. His hooks had penetrated deep and weren't going to be removed without a great deal of pain.

The woman stared at me expectantly.

"What would you like me to say, Miss Wise?" I

asked finally. "Yes, I work for Mr Ravens, but I have never ever heard the name Cressida Monroe. Not a whisper of it and so I don't really know what I could tell you."

She smiled at me. No doubt she considered her toothy grin ingratiating, but it simply made her round face look more moon-like. "I suspected you might offer that answer or variant of it. I didn't really expect you to actually know the girl. But," she raised her pen to her lips, "you are a person who can get in touch with Ravens. Perhaps the first person I've met who has a direct route. So, I want you, please, to pass on a few questions to him. Obviously, in my line of work, if I can avoid mentioning a man's name in the newspaper, I will try not to mention their name in the newspaper. But for that to happen, I will need answers. I'll need to understand what went on between Ravens and Miss Monroe. And I would obviously need to know when was the last time he saw her - alive."

The last word was left hanging, a spear hurled with force into a wall.

I nodded and ground my teeth simultaneously. "Do you want to write a list of questions and have me hand them to Mr Ravens? Or perhaps read them to him over the phone?"

"Yes," she said, her false perkiness reaching irritating dog whistle levels. "It would be a good start. I would be tremendously grateful. Although, obviously, I might have follow-up questions."

"I could do what you request," I said blithely. "But since Mr Ravens is actually in the country and I can take you to him this instant, I can actually do much better. Would you like to speak to him face-to-face?"

Her eyes widened. Right then there was a raucous

cheer from the other side of the bar. Whatever it was they'd been singing had obviously been a successful rendition.

"But he's in New York, isn't he?" she asked.

"No, no," I assured her. "He arrived three days ago. He's in London."

Her mouth made a perfect 'O'. "Really?" she said. "I spoke to his literary representative the day before Christmas Eve and he swore Mr Ravens was in America and would be there for the foreseeable. This is the reason I came after you. I heard from a contact that his man was Algernon Swafford and then this afternoon learned I could reach you here."

"Mr Ravens can be spontaneous." My tone was breezy. Probably unnaturally so, but the bar was too noisy for her to pick up on the fact. "So spontaneous in fact, those of us in his employ struggle to keep track of him. Actually, it's not only me checked into this hotel. Mr Ravens is here too. He's upstairs."

She goggled at me. Spluttered almost.

"Do you want to meet him?" I asked.

Of course she nodded enthusiastically.

I finished my rum in a gulp. Once more the effect was ephemeral. This damn English winter was making my bones feel much older than they were. Was this season always so excruciating? I struggled to recall properly. My childhood seemed a black and white memory, while my life in Los Angeles was Technicolor. It's fair to say, for me, the monochrome of the distant past was never warm.

"I'm sure he'll be happy to answer your questions. He prides himself on his good name" – which was a lie and she undoubtedly knew it was a lie – "and I'm sure he'll be pleased to have the opportunity to clarify matters." I stood and held my hand graciously to her. "Shall we?"

Her fingers were chilled, but her smile was warm, full and stupidly grateful. I led her the few steps out of the bar – rescuing us both from another singsong starting up – and into the deserted lobby. There were no comfortable places to wait in this English hotel. In fact, the lobby was basically a cloakroom with a register and corridor. I guided her through it towards the staircase (my countrymen hadn't reached the stage where they regularly employed elevators, it seemed). Opening the heavy door and letting her go first into the cold stairwell. Every inch the chivalrous gent, almost.

"We're the second floor," I said.

She waited on the bottom step, until I moved around her blue, square bulk to take the lead. Clearly she was trying to compose herself. This was such an unexpected development for the evening, she was trying to make it seem she was prepared for it.

I had to stop myself chuckling.

"What's he like?" she asked suddenly, as we rounded the first flight.

"He's unpredictable as the young often are and brash as the young often are. But he can be charming as well."

Her lips pursed, considering. "And how is he with difficult questions?"

"Disarming,"

Room 212 was the door we stopped at and it was right next to mine. More's the bloody pity.

I raised my hand to knock, but then grinned, thinking better of it. "I won't announce you," I whispered, "Mr Ravens is a man who despises artificial formality."

Instead I opened the door a crack. Inside it was dark, seemingly lit by one bedside lamp.

Her eyes peered to mine, trusting, and yet with a sudden nervousness apparent through her determinedly perky Scots exterior.

Then I called: "Mr Ravens. There's a visitor for you!"

The journalist's chin jutted forward and with her notepad primed in hand, she stepped past me into the darkness. It was then the Callicantzaros clamped its jaw around her neck and ripped her throat open before she could scream.

CHAPTER TWO

One comes across all kinds of darkness when associated with Jacob Ravens. But this had turned my stomach from the first instant it was thrust upon me. A Callicantzaros is a Greek vampire and quite the ugliest creature you could ever wish to see. Its skin is shrivelled to a coal black, its eyes are a dull and nasty red (except when its blood is hot, then they burn with fury) while its jaw is so elongated it resembles a kind of monstrous rodent. The limbs and body of this creature are so stretched and distorted you could imagine it had spent time on some infernal wrack. The result is its legs are long like an insect's and its arms can swing in wide arcs and are sharpened from the elbow into jagged claws.

Apparently they spend most of their time in hibernation and a myth has been constructed around them that they only emerge between Christmas and New Year. So, rather than an orange in the stocking, there are those of us unfortunate enough to receive this devilish creature.

I didn't care to learn of its habits, but this is what I found myself doing. Christmas Eve I received one of those muffled phone calls from another flunky of Ravens. With an unpleasant relish in his voice, he told me I was going to be having a guest delivered at half past eleven at night. That she would arrive in a crate and be placed in the room next to mine. My task was to make sure the room stayed dark and she was provided with enough to eat. A victim a day should suffice. Or maybe every other day, should pickings be scarce.

Every job I took for the man shrunk my soul further and tortured my sense of self, but there was no way I could refuse.

I feared hunting down people to feed this foul creature was going to be a time consuming task. Tonight, well, the thought of what I'd done didn't dampen my spirits even slightly. The Scottish bint had deserved it. Maybe her presenting herself to me in this fashion meant my luck was finally turning.

Quite what Ravens wanted with such a creature, or why he desired me to look after it, was anyone's guess. Perhaps she had meant something to him when she was human, or possibly he was doing it for nothing but sport. In my grim weariness, I never roused myself to ask questions. After all, the answers were bound to be worse than I could ever imagine.

Once upon a time, I had been in charge of my own destiny. One of those champions in life who leave others in their wake. A man of comfortable means; a man to be admired. Algernon Swafford belongs to no man, I'd tell people, and no truer words had ever been spoken. It cost fifty dollars a day to hire me; more if you wanted my extra special service. And I was worth every cent. I was the man kings of industry called, I was in movie stars' rolodexes (or at least their managers'). I was important. Then I accepted an assignment to find and eliminate the horror author Jacob Ravens.

All I knew about him was that he was a roué and a grade-A bounder. Your standard heartless bastard. It was when I tracked him to a nothing town on the California coast that I realised the truth. Jacob Ravens was the devil in human form. He was beyond evil, a force of pure blackness. I'd gone there to pull the trigger on him, but instead all my mettle was crushed by his will. I'd been a strong man, a man of substance, never bullied by anybody – but after half an hour with him I was, I'm ashamed to say, a snivelling wreck. Right there and then I tried to kill myself. A brutal act I never imagined I'd consider. Desperately I put a gun to my head and pulled the trigger, but through an act of dreadful magic he stopped the bullet.

Then – the most horrific punishment – he made me his man. His servant. His retainer. His slave. I have to do his bidding or face eternal torment.

Left to my own will, I would never have set foot in Britain. Never gone home. Maybe that was the reason it gave Ravens such pleasure to send me here, in the cold and dark of winter as well. And to rile me, it seemed, he sent a literal monster for me to look after. A disgusting specimen he must have known would make me physically sick to look upon.

Not that anyone else would understand the fact. I wear a mask which appears unruffled to the outside world and I try to take everything in my stride now. After all, I'm never going to meet a greater monster than Jacob Ravens, am I?

Lying on my lumpy hotel room mattress, the sounds of slurping and feeding coming faintly through the wall, I tried to imagine what this creature was before she too encountered Ravens. I pictured her as a beautiful young lady, a good daughter – virginal and a Christian. There's a chance the curse was always upon her, but I think what happened to her was the direct result of meeting Jacob Ravens. I always blame him.

Never in my life did I think I'd spend the night of Christmas Day hiring a bow legged streetwalker with bad teeth. How could I imagine I'd actually escort such a wench and listen to her estuary prattling without losing my temper? What had I become that I could make this woman – whose name I deliberately didn't ask – feel safe as I led her to her painful death?

Tomorrow (or maybe I'd leave it to the day after), it was going to be someone else. Another person – a woman, more than likely – who was going to wake up, relatively blameless in life and looking forward to a future. Instead she would be fed to a creature who would almost decapitate her with its first sally and then loudly and angrily suck every drop of the resultant blood.

What made the whole thing more galling, was that this wasn't my main purpose in London. I had wondered why I had been sent to this grey wreck of a city, but a second phone call, an hour after the first, had made it a little clearer. I had an appointment the following morning to meet Emilia Ravens. Mrs Jacob Ravens herself.

CHAPTER THREE

Mrs Emilia Ravens, the errant wife.

I had never ever laid eyes on her before, but the stories I'd heard had it that she was incredibly beautiful. Although, if the stories were correct, a bit too Latina in looks for my taste – even if she was by birth an English woman. How pretty the picture didn't really matter. She was no doubt lovely to gaze at, but apparently she was as depraved as her husband. In marrying her, he had met his match in debasement.

The following morning, after another night where I passed into numbed unconsciousness rather than sleep, I put on the best suit I'd brought with me – navy and double breasted – and a matching tie which I wound in a Windsor knot. I did think of wearing my fedora, but didn't want to stand out too much. The hats in this city were nowhere near as expensive as mine. They were boxy and functional and ugly as a brick. My head would just have to get cold.

She, I was informed, was staying at the Ritz. I may have considered the hotel I was in might – for its many flaws – be one of the better ones in London, but there was always a next level. Not only had she checked into

London's fanciest and most expensive hotel, when I arrived I learned she had managed to clear the tearoom entirely for our meeting. The small paper sign outside said it was closed for a private party, but it was only me and her and didn't feel much like any party at all.

The obsequiousness with which the porter greeted me and took me to the doorway suggested a large amount of money was being spent by this guest, or else he was already besotted by her.

Despite myself, although I didn't want to, I took a sharp intake of breath when I saw her. She was as magnificently beautiful as everyone said. And the forthright way she instantly met my gaze – not bashful or blushing; nothing so demure – suggested she damn well knew it.

Back when I'd first moved to Los Angeles, there was a Mexican girl who danced in a speakeasy where various low-lifes congregated. This young woman wasn't my type at all – too easy – but objectively it was clear she was a knockout. Long legs, perfect figure, a doll like face with smooth skin and an upturned nose. There was a confidence to her, in the way she moved and posed. The way she flicked her long, thick hair so it fell effortlessly to her shoulders. I suppose she was only about nineteen and had the allure of youth and what they these days call sex appeal. As I say, she wasn't my kind of dish and I probably spoke no more than three dozen words to her in our entire acquaintance, but I remember her as the pinnacle of a certain type of desirability.

That image was replaced right there and then by Emilia Ravens. Not only was she the same mix of sensuality and beauty, she had a sense of poise to her – a certain English refinement – which the poor Mexican girl was never going to manage. Simply sat there – her gaze unswerving – she exuded more attraction than the Mex did while flicking up her skirts.

As I was shown into that large tearoom at eleven on the dot (a room which had seemingly not altered since my Aunt took me there for tea nearly fifty years earlier), she sat at a round table, on the other side. There was no cake in front of her, but she did have a cup of steaming coffee. Her flickering wide dark brown eyes fixed on me – taking my measure – and I did my best to walk across to her calmly, a man without any excitement in his blood. It had been awhile since I'd had a dalliance with a woman and – if I'm honest – a while since I'd had any real stirrings. I didn't want her to suspect she was causing the latter and given me thoughts of the former.

Languidly she took a sip of her coffee. She was dressed in a tailor made black suit – French fashions, I would have guessed – with a pillbox hat perched at a slight angle above her dark hair. Despite being pertly sat and partly hidden by a tablecloth, I couldn't help but be awed at the sheer perfection of her figure. It was impossible not to notice and imagine her long legs and svelte form, even with my gaze lost in the feline-esque perfection of her face.

Around her neck was a choker necklace and a large ruby which was pressed tight to her throat. The gem was so bright, it made up for a lack of dazzling smile in my direction. It also looked uncomfortable sat there, so close to her white skin it was a wonder she could breathe. But then rumour had it that she was a woman who enjoyed a bit of discomfort from time to time.

I tried a charming smile for her when I reached the table, but it was not reciprocated. All I saw in her gaze was coolness. Her eyes were dark naturally, nearly all iris, but there wasn't an ounce of warmth in them. Why would she offer me the courtesy? I was her husband's servant, his catspaw, and I was old and grey. Why would this young woman, seemingly barely into the radiance of her twenties, look at meeting me as anything other than an inconvenience?

"So you must be Swafford then?" she said. Her tone deeply unimpressed.

I had brought myself to a stop at the chair in front of her and I nodded once. "At your service, Mrs Ravens."

Her hand flicked her dark hair from her forehead. "Jacob told me once you were a character. That despite being this stiff Englishman, you were an American at heart. You know us expats over there go one of two ways. There are those who are forward looking and embrace the country and seize the opportunity. They become more American than the Americans themselves. Then there are those who hang onto the past with all their might. Who set their clocks to Greenwich Mean Time and take tea and moan about how every single thing isn't exactly the same as Blighty would make it. Well, Jacob said if I were to ever meet you, I'd no doubt think you were the latter, when instead you were the former. A go getter wrapped in a fusty tweed coat."

The old me would have turned on his heel if someone – anyone – spoke to him in such a way. Certainly if that slander had come from a bint who every rumour suggested was no better than she ought to be, I'd have unleashed my outrage. Now though she was my boss's (my master's) wife and I had to stand there and take it. Smile at her besmirching me with the epithet "fusty".

"Sit!" she ordered. To her I was nothing more than the houseboy and one who was due to be reprimanded.

Slowly, portraying myself as less of a captive than I actually was, I pulled out the chair in front of her. Trying forlornly to give the impression there remained a spark inside me.

From the corner of my eye, I espied a spotless waiter at the far corner of the room, discreetly distanced from earshot. She didn't beckon him to bring me a cup of coffee though.

Instead she lit a cigarette and blew out slowly and coolly. "How are you finding London, Swafford?"

"Much as I expected," I said, wearily. "Cold, dark and broken."

She gave a light and airy chuckle. If I hadn't been so tense and on guard of myself, I might have fallen a little in love with the sound. "That it is! That it is! I'm from Highgate myself. The house in which I was born isn't there any longer. I can't say the knowledge of its sudden absence makes me regretful. Good riddance to it! Is this your first return visit?"

I nodded.

"I find America very invigorating." Her speech was direct and an almost irresistible light flashed suddenly in her eyes. "I appreciate it. But I'm always more drawn to Europe. If it wasn't for my marriage, I'd find an apartment in Barcelona and stay there forever. Have passionate affairs with every bullfighter I could find."

There was nothing I could say to that. I'd been to Europe in the trenches and had no intention of paying a return visit, while the idea of congress with Spaniards filled me with revulsion. I kept my mask impassive, it's what it was there for.

"How's Jacob's little guest?" she asked.

I shuddered. "I'm doing what was asked of me. I'm keeping her discreetly safe and I'm keeping her fed."

"And you haven't enquired how she is? Whether or not she's enjoying her London experience?"

"No. I value my life too much for such foolhardiness."

"Glad to hear it." The flatness of her voice made obvious she couldn't really care what happened to my existence.

Her gaze was appraising for a good minute. She tapped the ash of her cigarette onto the floor, not caring that there was a perfectly good and expensive ashtray on the table. The waiter in the corner stayed as stony faced as a king's guard. Possibly his lack of movement, or polite coughed reprimand, was to spite the poor sod who'd have to make everything pristine again before the luncheon crowd was let in.

"You realise she's not the main reason you're here, don't you?"

"I gathered as much," I said.

"Jacob wants you to go and meet someone."

"Someone who isn't you?"

She laughed prettily. "Things are frequently awful between Jacob and me, and we do often resort to intermediaries, but I don't think he's developed quite the level of hatred for me yet that he'd send his ruthless enforcer six thousand miles to deal with me."

"Who then?" I asked.

"His name is Maximillian Belloc. You might have heard of him, he's a concert pianist."

I shook my head.

"Oh well, I'm sure his publicist will be broken apart at your ignorance. He won't be hard to find and, for a man of your talents, not hard to get an audience with."

"An audience about what?"

"About whether he means Jacob any harm."

"And if he does?"

She laughed one more time. "Then Jacob wants you to do what you do, Mr Swafford. He wants you to kill him."

The two of us stared at each other, me flicking my gaze to that waiter to make sure he was still stony faced and unhearing.

As I did, she leant forward and purred almost seductively: "As well as fusty, my husband also claimed you were a tough guy. Maybe we should put this to the test soon, don't you think?"

It's possible my mouth did open a little, but I didn't ask her what she meant.

CHAPTER FOUR

As she said, Maximillian Belloc wasn't hard to find. On a teak table in the grand Ritz hotel reception on my exit, I espied a pile of small black and white flyers advertising his concert tonight. It was too much of a coincidence and so I guessed another flunky of Ravens had left it there for me to stumble across. Another move in this game I was forced to play.

The recital was highlights of Grieg and Debussy and he was playing at The Mallory Hall. Like The Ritz, it was a venue I remembered from my childhood. Indeed, unlike The Ritz, I had been there more than once. It was one of the few excursions where it was solely my father and I. We went there on numerous occasions to see his favourite violinist. The name of that particular gentleman eludes me and – if I'm honest – I have never had much of an ear for music, but I remember he was a corpulent man who dripped perspiration onto his bow. The venue itself was on High Holborn and impressively huge. It was also easily missed. Being a doorway and a ticket office above ground, with no real clue as to how cavernous the hall beneath was. Its subterranean nature meant it was completely unaffected by the Blitz. No doubt thousands of cockney types sheltered there night after night from the doodlebugs, people who wouldn't recognise Debussy from a ham sandwich.

When I marched there that lunchtime, I discovered there were a few tickets left for the night's performance. I purchased mine from the whey faced West Country girl they had manning the desk, but of course having a ticket in my possession didn't guarantee me any kind of private audience.

So I got there early in the evening – a good hour before the concert was scheduled to start – and spoke to the same slightly dim Bristol girl (who appeared to me as if she'd be more comfortable, and competent, milking a cow). I told her I wanted to see Mr Belloc and she regarded me blankly to the point of slack-jawed. Russian or Turkish might as well have been spewing from between my lips. Finally the words seemed to penetrate her skull and she hesitantly replied, in her squeaky voice, that there were a couple of tickets left to watch him play. I merely smiled, my mask giving every impression I wasn't irritated to my core by her, and said I was a journalist. The LA Times, I proclaimed, and that despite me not having made any prior arrangements, it would be great to have a few words

Despite the fact I didn't have a press pass (which I intended to explain by averring they weren't needed in more forward thinking America), the word 'journalist' made her spring into life. Or as much vitality as the girl was ever going to have. A colleague of hers was sauntering past – a boy, younger than her, barely shaving – and she asked him to fetch Mr Partridge. Told him I was with the press.

I had no idea who this Mr Partridge was, didn't know if I wanted to speak with him, but I managed to smile appreciatively.

It didn't take long for Mr Partridge to trot up the stairs – which was good as the girl and I were getting bored looking at each other – and a more unprepossessing man in a more unprepossessing suit I have scarcely ever met. A short, rotund yeoman type with receding hair which he had still gone to the trouble of running a pint of oil through. There was a sheen of sweat to him and he was a little breathless, suggesting he had run to see me. But then he was one of those men who appeared to be always sweating. It probably oozed from him while he slept. His unfortunate pores made his choice of a linen mustard suit seem more foolhardy. Not only was it ill-fitting, but a man should only wear such a suit if he is positive he can keep himself cool. In the cold depths of an English winter, this man was most definitely failing. I could almost see the odours and moisture of his fat body seeping into the material.

When he opened his mouth, I was surprised by his strong Northumberland accent. To look at him, one would imagine he was an East End Jew with an anglicised name. That didn't seem to be the case.

He held out his hand, as moist as the rest of him, and I cringed inside as I shook it.

"Partridge is the name, my friend. They tell me you're the fourth estate." He spoke in a fast rhythm, as if reciting the words of a song. "What can I do for you?"

I let go of his hand with relief. "I'd like to have a few words with Mr Belloc, if I may." My manner was as polite and inoffensive as it could possibly be. "A short interview, perhaps."

He crinkled his brow. "No can do, mate. Mr Belloc is an artiste and thus he has very few dealings with the popular press. We did have a luncheon with the toffs at The Daily Telegraph at the start of this tour, but that's it."

"Oh, I'll be quick," I said. "I'll be out of his hair well before he starts playing."

"What? You want to speak to him now?"

I nodded.

"Oh no, no." He shook his head fulsomely. "There's no way he can make time for an interview *before* a performance. He has to prepare himself, don't you see? These artistes are delicate creatures – little greenhouse flowers, they are – and it wouldn't do for him to be disturbed. It may affect the quality of his performance."

"Afterwards, then."

"Afterwards?" He chuckled, my request apparently being akin to me suggesting an arm-wresting competition for Belloc with the Aga Khan. "No, no. Afterwards is when these artistes are at their most delicate. They're worried about whether the standing ovation wasn't long enough, or if they didn't hit the right note at one point in the third movement. It can even be whether an audience member was staring at them funny. I'm afraid it simply isn't feasible to start chatting two to the dozen to the press afterwards. Maybe, when the tour is winding to a close, when the pressures on Mr Belloc have subsided to a more comfortable level, you can speak to him then."

"And when will that be?" I asked.

"March" was his blunt reply, with a little smile which was half apology and half mocking.

"Please." I opened my arms and grinned ingratiatingly. "I don't know if it's been mentioned to you, but I'm from The Los Angeles Times. I have come a long way."

His eyes bulged a little with surprise. "Yes, the boy mentioned it, but I guessed he was mistaken. That it was The Luton Times, or a different provincial rag. Excuse my French, but why the hell would The Los Angeles bloody Times be interested in Mr Belloc? We don't have any concert dates planned for America."

"News of great musicianship will always spread fast."

He chewed his tongue around in his mouth and regarded me top to bottom. Taking in what a good, well-made, unstained suit looked like. "I'm sorry," he said. "I forget my manners occasionally, what did you say your name was?"

"My name is Algernon Swafford."

The change in him was instant. From a sweaty ball manning a blockade, his posture became immediately more deferent – worshipful even. His shoulders sunk a little. In a mere few seconds, I was a man he wasn't sure he could meet in the eye.

Partridge coughed politely. "Well, yes, you being you rather puts a different complexion on matters, doesn't it? Obviously it changes things a little. Of course Mr Belloc will want to see you. I will take you to him forthwith."

I regarded him coolly, not wanting to show any surprise.

"You've heard my name then?"

He had already taken a few steps to the staircase, but then shuffled towards me. After a nervous glance around he leant in close enough I could smell his fetid odour, then – almost in a whisper – asked: "Are you sure you want to do this?"

"I'm sure." Perhaps I should have considered the question more, but I was past the point where I had any choice.

"Fine," he said with false cheerfulness. "I'll take you to him."

He led the way with stooped shoulders as I moved smoothly behind him. At my left breast was a Remington I'd purchased for a reasonable price from a dubious individual in Soho. I was ready.

CHAPTER FIVE

Once upon a time, I only killed men who I was sure deserved it. Bastards who had lived terrible lives and had their untimely fate coming to them. Then I met Jacob Ravens and I started to kill for him.

The first man he had had me execute was a barber on the island of Manhattan. Seemingly a kindly old gent who had built a successful business for himself on 22nd Street, while raising his son and daughter, having been widowed at a young age. To me, he seemed as inoffensive an individual who ever lived. He even stayed open a little later when I arrived at closing time to give me a shave and a haircut in the empty barbershop. When I paid him by blowing his brains through the top of his skull, the surprised look on his face showed he was as shocked by his fate as anybody else. He had no inkling it was coming. Zero idea what he'd actually done. Or maybe he hadn't really done anything at all and it was simply a dark jape. Only Jacob Ravens knew for sure.

That was the first of my victims for Ravens. There have been so, so many since.

Rolls of fat jiggling in his suit, Partridge led me

down the stairs, through a long corridor winding around the concert hall itself and into an empty room. I guessed it was a dressing room and that every door along the corridor led to a similarly cramped space. If there had been a whole orchestra playing, the entire area would have teemed with activity. As it was a solo performance, it was empty and echoing and I was left to stare at the grey walls alone.

If I could have walked away right then, I would have.

Something about this clearly wasn't right. Nothing I ever did for Ravens felt correct, but I was particularly uneasy about this. It was an anxiety I couldn't describe, which I had no way of putting my finger on. Mostly, when I got my orders, I gritted my teeth and got on with it. Pointed the gun and pulled the trigger in whichever direction it was wanted. But right then – alone in the ugly, grey, poky room – a wave of sickening nervousness swept over me.

The fear I'd had for a long while that my true self was slipping away became overwhelming. Every day I worked for Ravens, every blood soaked task I undertook for him, made me feel a little less like me. I was no longer the Algernon Swafford who belonged to no man, I was a damned slave unable to refuse any instruction, no matter how repellent. But right there and then, waiting for this man Belloc with iron in my suit, the sensation was the most intense I'd ever felt. It wasn't merely the fear I was slipping away from myself, it was the dread I had already gone.

I shuddered when I heard the footsteps marching down the endless corridor. A booming thud which smacked repeatedly into my skull. Approaching, yet somehow already seeming right outside the door.

Suddenly I felt terrified down to my marrow. I didn't know who I was and I was desperate to escape everything. To run and hide from this man charging towards me, to escape from Ravens himself. The gun beneath my shoulder might as well have been a child's toy, I didn't feel big or brave enough to use it.

My neck turned my head slowly. A trembling gaze towards the door and the resounding footfalls. I tried not to let my mouth slacken or my eyes burst wide. But I could feel the cold perspiration on my forehead and knew my fingers were shaking embarrassingly.

Then the door flew open – kicked asunder – and the man appeared.

I took a deep gulp.

Part of it was relief. In the flesh he was short, slight and older than I was. He was not an obvious monster, he was a little man – one I could easily take in any battle. There was a gasp of surprise. Of anti-climax, even. The Algernon Swafford who had tumbled with half a dozen of the nastiest hoodlums in Los Angeles, feeling sure of himself again.

That confidence lasted only a few seconds.

As I took him in fully – weedy in his grey suit – I realised this was a person, exactly like Ravens. A man to be dreadfully afeard of.

Part of it was the expression he wore: such brutal and righteous condemnation I'd never encountered before. But mostly it was his presence. This somebody who, the same as Ravens, exuded a spectral and *other* kind of power. One I could instantly recognise. I knew from painful experience that such individuals were able to take control of even the strongest and most determinedly wilful.

"Swafford!" he barked, an angry statement rather

than a question.

In dime-store novels and conveyer belt movies, detectives are always spouting scintillating dialogue. Right then, any attempt at wit was beyond me and all I could do was squeak my answer.

"Yes."

"Do you know who I am?"

"Belloc," I swallowed

He nodded once and sneered. His English was exemplary, but his voice had an exotic European accent. I couldn't place it, but it was probably one of those Iron Curtain countries.

"Did Mister Jacob Ravens send you?"

"He did."

"Why?"

"To find out if you can hurt him."

"And if I can?"

My voice wavered. "Then I should kill you."

"Are you carrying a firearm upon your person?"

"Yes."

"And do you want to kill me?"

"I've been ordered to."

"But what do you want, Swafford?"

My mouth opened, but I couldn't answer the question.

At last Belloc raised the corners of his lips, condescendingly, a schoolmaster confronted by his dimmest pupil. "Fine," he spoke slowly. "I understand the true picture of things as they are and I think a little re-education might be in order."

What happened next was so astounding I can hardly credit it, but it seemed that from thin air a large white snow leopard appeared. This giant beast regarded me for a second with hungry eyes and slavering lips and then sunk its teeth deep into my flesh.

CHAPTER SIX

I flinched in my seat, but it was useless. This was a small room and this beast was much bigger than I. Before I could believe it was there, the leopard had clamped its teeth around my shoulder and sunk its claws into my belly. I felt my innards puncture and the blood spray from my wounds. With a feline grunt it tore me from the seat. This impossible beast was huge, slobbering and strangely scentless. Like the ghost of a wild animal rendered into corporeal form. The leopard's jaw let go and I gasped, not out of the cessation of pain, but because my blood sprayed faster. Slicking onto its white coat. With its eyes dead, but its mouth so alive and ravenous, this all too real apparition peered at me and licked its crimson stained lips. Then it sank the whole cavern of its mouth onto my face.

From youth I'd taught myself to be brave. I had served with honour in the trenches of the Somme. Afterwards I'd won commendations for my work in the Metropolitan Police Force. I had then thrown in everything I'd ever had and made the gamble of moving to America. Sailing to New York without a single friendly face awaiting me, then making my way slowly across the country. Settling in Los Angeles when parts of it remained dirt tracks and farmland. It had been a glittering, if onerous career. I had faced off against gangsters, cops and hitmen, and I had done it all without showing a molecule of fear.

Now I wept. Nothing more than a pathetic little girl. My death wasn't with honour or bravery or decency, it was as a damn coward.

I squirmed on the floor, the tiles soaked with my own blood, and I realised with shame and a sensation of squelchy dampness that I'd soiled myself.

There was blackness and I knew that I had died. I was certain of it. It was the nothing of a void. I hadn't gone to heaven and I wasn't in charge of my own destiny enough to warrant hell. Instead I was going to float in blankness for eternity.

Around me was darkness. I could feel nothing. And after the inexplicable big cat and the weak way I'd died, it actually felt so good I almost gave a little laugh.

Then a voice burst from nowhere.

Belloc's voice.

And at the sound of it, I almost screamed

"I can be your saviour or your destroyer!" It roared at me.

I squirmed in the darkness. My sense of physicality had gone, drifted to nothing in the void, but right then I think I speckled my shirtfront with vomit. I had only vomited twice in my life. A fact I was immensely proud of. But in my death it was almost the first thing I did.

Squinting, I imagined I saw a shadowy form. Belloc himself, but bigger and more powerful. He was all around me, not a visitor in the void like I was, but the void itself.

"Do you understand me?" he snarled. There was no

comfort to his tone, it burst all around me – coming from every direction – with sheer contempt. "You are at a train station. One of the trains on the platform is an express heading towards your redemption, the other is the slow train to your doom. Which are you going to choose to take?"

He didn't wait for me to answer the question.

"Quite the reputation you had until recently. You were a man to be trusted, one who got things done. It's that man I need today. If he is in there, it's that man I need to summon forth. Jacob is right, I do mean him harm. But to do so, I am going to need your help. Are you still the man who can help me?"

He paused dramatically before his voice finally boomed: "I need you to kill Jacob!"

I think I whimpered. What he offered was my deepest desire, my most hidden wish, but the sound which escaped my lips was a muffled shriek.

The voice echoed all around me. "You understand what Jacob is, don't you? The man is a servant to demons and anyone who dedicates their life to him is in thrall to those same demons. I am offering you the chance to leave the side of darkness and come to the righteous. I am giving you the opportunity to redeem yourself with the angels, but is there enough of you in your beating breast to do that?"

My mouth opened, but no sounds came forth.

Belloc's voice didn't wait for a response. "I realise he has made you his pet, that he has bound you to him in a million different ways. But I am offering you the chance to smash those bonds, to free yourself. Are you a man who can take this opportunity?"

Finally I managed to utter words, although they were so meek, they were instantly swallowed by the void. "I can't."

"Think of who you were!" the voice bellowed. "A Los Angeles private detective who anybody of any importance in that fine city knew. And consider what you've become, a pandering wretch. A pathetic wreck of a human being. Break those bonds, reaffirm yourself. Rediscover the man you once were and let us destroy the filth of Jacob together."

"I can't."

I wanted to. With all which remained within me, I wanted to. Jacob Ravens was a loathsome example of a man. A sodomite, an adulterer, a cheat, a liar, a thief, a cold-blooded murderer. And those were just the crimes within reach of any normal human being. There were also those which defied comprehension. So many other wicked acts he'd committed beyond the laws of God and nature.

Yet still I couldn't. Despite what I had become and how all I did in his service revolting me, I couldn't find a way to do anything to hurt him. No matter how much I craved to feel his throat in my hands.

"Help me!" screamed the voice of Belloc.

"I can't."

I was blubbing. It was too late, there was nothing of the old me left.

Suddenly, all the wounds the large cat had inflicted tore open painfully and my blood spewed forth again. I could feel my body ripping apart, the leopard materialising within me and tearing wildly at my insides.

"Concentrate!" Belloc's voice yelled, and it was the only thing around me which didn't cause me pain. "Remember who you are. Grab hold of your true colours!"

The void fell from the blackness to white – time itself bent and screamed – then I was in the trenches, in the crumpled brown of my uniform.

In the distance was the rattle of German machinegun fire, the tang of cordite forever in the air. Below my feet was the endlessly damp soil, boots stamping on the overflowing piss and shit of the inexpertly built latrines. It was horrible and disgusting and I'm not sure anyone, no matter how brave a man they were, ever got used to it.

I'd been proud of myself in The Great War. How I had stood tall as a man and done my bit, resolute in never ever buckling under. I awoke each morning and knew there were ten thousand Hun close by and they were determined to kill me. That they were going to fire their guns and shoot off their bombs and their sole intention was to murder me and the brave men of my platoon. But I was never going to let those German bastards have the satisfaction of me showing the slightest fear. I would fight to my last bullet and the final thrust of bayonet. If they wanted to kill me, then they could come and get me, but I would send dozens of them to their own unmarked graves first.

But in this new memory, I was prostrate on the effluence-soaked floor of the trench, one of those sobbing pale faced boys who earned contempt and pity in equal measure. A useless sissy who never slept at night because he was too busy weeping for his mummy. A worthless child who the platoon would have to wrestle over the wall of the trench and who was only good as cannon fodder.

Horribly it was me now.

The piss and excrement wasn't beneath my feet, it was smeared onto my face. One of my commanding officers had been so disgusted by me, he had actually shoved me to the bottom of the trench. Used his foot to grind my mouth into the muck in an attempt to make me become a man. It hadn't worked. All of the other boys and men spat and sneered at me. They hated me and I hated myself. But there was nothing I could do about it. Whenever the opposition fired a bullet, I didn't put my jaw out and face it, instead I cowered and wished I could be in safe Blighty. At my core I was a gutless coward and I knew I deserved the kicks and punches they gave me. Undoubtedly I had earned the white feathers they'd pinned to my chest.

For this version of me, after the war wasn't much better. Talk of my cowardice had reached my father and he was as revolted as everybody else. I needed to convalesce, but there was no chance of that happening near my family. I was sent to the north, far from home, left to pull myself together without ever seeing a friendly face.

I did apply for the police after the war, but I was rejected. A couple of my fellow soldiers had beaten me to it and word of my yellow streak had already made it around. I imagine they laughed at my impudence and then crumpled my letter into rubbish.

The notion never occurred that I should cross The Atlantic, that I could leave it all behind and start a new life. I had this naive idea fixed in mind that I was going to show everybody. Prove to my father I was worthy. Despite everything, I was a good son who deserved respect.

But of course I didn't. Through a friend of mine from school, who'd never really liked me, I got the job at an East End collections agency. A shabby little business run by a shabby little Irishman. Hardly the occupation for a one such as I. My day's work took me to see old ladies who owed rent, as well as mothers whose husbands had absconded and stranded them with debts. There was nothing honourable to it, but I was too worthless to think of any other way to earn a living.

Until one day in spring 1936, this debased livelihood went wrong for me. It should have been a simple assignment: knocking the door of a man who had bought furniture on credit and wasn't paying his debt. Except that man's cousin was a gangster named Eddie Hawk, and this Eddie Hawk was the only one home when I rang the doorbell and already in a bad mood. Shamefully, I didn't offer any fight when he whipped a razor from his trouser pocket and slashed open my face. I did nothing to stop him as he blinded me. My last sight in the world? Him laughing hysterically at my spilled blood.

The rest of my days were spent in the same convalescence home in the north. I literally couldn't see any friendly faces, not that anyone bothered to visit. Years went past and I lived as a nothing, a shell. Word reached me that both my parents had died and left me a small allowance. The fees on the home though were going to swallow all the money. At the end of it I'd have no resources and no roof above my head. A blind wreck of a man who nobody was going to do a single favour for.

And the most horrible thing was that, deep within, I knew I deserved it. I was a cowardly wretch and this was the end which was always meant to come to me.

CHAPTER SEVEN

The music resembled a lullaby. So soothing and tranquil.

Bathed in one bright spotlight, Belloc sat on the stage in front of me, dressed to the nines. His expression transfixed by his own fingers dancing on the keyboard. One could imagine each of them was its own miniature Fred Astaire, waltzing away on the blacks and whites. And the music rose so clear from the large, white grand piano. Resounding, as it lulled me into calmness.

On another day, in different circumstances, it would have been wonderful – even for a man such as I who had only a passing interest in music – to watch him and hear what he played. Now I felt sick and discombobulated.

I had no idea how I got there, no clue how I'd arrived in the auditorium, but I had a seat right at the centre. The light shone on him, but it also seemed to reflect onto me. So I was watching him up there, but he was also able to see me. Thus – as my senses settled to near normal and I felt deep breaths come into my lungs – I smiled and drummed my fingers on my thighs, to show him I was enjoying it. It was important to me all of a sudden that he understood the fact. The music was beautiful. As I tried to put myself back together, I appreciated his performance was heavenly.

There were disconcerting flashes of the leopard in my mind, and I felt myself somewhat fragmented after the void; but they resembled more the memories of dreams, rather than actual flesh-and-blood memories. Still my banging on my thighs served to both show Belloc that I was appreciating his recital and to prove to myself I was re-assembled. My legs were in the right place, my hands and arms were in the right place. Each of my ears were where they should be at the side of my head. I could actually feel my heart beat its own gentle rhythm and with it a calmness washed over me.

The music burst louder. In an instant it felt like Belloc's grand piano had a dozen other pianos echoing it, a whole piano orchestra consisting of only genius musicians. My eyes opened wide and the music poured into me. All other thoughts thrown roughly out of my mind. There was only the music and it filled my senses. Billowing its way into me and eliminating everything else.

Sat there at the centre of the hall, it seemed he was playing only for me.

Maybe he was. It was a sensation both half flattering and half dreadful – that this entire concert was a private one for me. Which is why I was illuminated by a sliver of his spotlight, I was the only person who mattered. Belloc was filling the emptiness of my soul with beautiful sounds. In this auditorium, in the entire universe, I was the lone individual who mattered.

And I was grasping hold of his talent. I have never been a devotee of records and certainly did not own any kind of player. The only radio I possessed was in my car. In the past I had been to concerts, but they were largely work related – in fact the last I went to was one of the first West Coast shows of the young Frank Sinatra. That's how long ago it was.

No, it was wrong of me to think of other performers. Certainly not that licentious Italian runt. All stray thoughts were bombarded from my mind by the wondrous sounds from under Belloc's fingers.

I felt safe. Genuinely that's the sense which washed over me: safe and looked after for the first time in years.

As casually as I could, I tried to take in the auditorium. Not wanting to shift my gaze from the spotlight, or my attention from his playing, but needing to understand my surroundings. To know this was really all for me.

It seemed hard however for me to move my head either left or right. To take my eyes off Belloc and his rhythmic hands and the melodies so beautiful. The sight of him performing was a thing of such grace. Who'd have imagined this unimposing, little man possessed this quantity of elegance? Finally as he reached a quieter – but still so moving – passage, I was able to glance to the left.

There were no other people there.

Same if I looked to my right.

My fingers drummed my thighs a bit more heartily, trying to focus only on the concerto, on what made me happy.

The seats beside me – the seats the entire length of the row, in both directions – were occupied. They just weren't occupied by people. Each of them was filled by one of those plastic mannequins which the finer boutiques in Hollywood and Bel Air display in their windows. They were still and lifeless and dressed in old clothing. The fashions of my police years in London – sharp suits and cocktail dresses. More than one of them had been posed so they had unlit cigarettes raised close to their lips. But there was no animation to them, no life, I might as well have been sharing the concert hall with a thousand dead bodies.

Shaken, I gazed to Belloc on the stage.

The music burst louder, filling me up. My hands beat fast against my thighs, my head nodded along. There was a little smile on his face as I tried to think only of his playing. What did the smile mean? I'd realised this concert was for me. Was he pleased by the fact?

As the tune progressed though, it didn't matter. Whatever this piece was called, whether it was Debussy or Grieg, he reached a particularly beautiful passage. It burst into me and lifted my soul and removed everything else. All I could do was sit there enraptured, while all fear was wiped from me.

CHAPTER EIGHT

"Tell me," said Belloc. "How are you feeling?"

Without any recollection of the concert ending, I found myself in the dressing room. Belloc was in front of me, perched on the arm of the opposite chair with his tuxedo undone and his bowtie flapping from his collar.

There was a thin stemmed cocktail glass in his hand and I wondered whether he might offer me a drink, but instead he sipped it himself.

"No!" He hammered the word forth with a Germanic bluntness. "I have a better question for you, Mr Swafford – not 'how are you', but 'who are you?'" He grinned at me. "I've been inside your mind and I've looked for the cowardly disgrace who has no more willpower than to do Jacob Ravens's bidding. I've hunted for this man in your memories, but I haven't found him, so tell me – who the hell are you?"

Without the music, everything seemed strange, but distant. That leopard clamping its jaws around while I was too helpless to defend myself. My cowardice in the trenches, my life trapped in London. This whole other existence which was never mine.

Fear and sickness rose within. I tried to hum the music to calm myself, but couldn't locate the memory of how it sounded anywhere in my mind. My hands gripped the side of my chair and I feared I was going to pitch forward. What stopped me was Belloc's eyes. Through force of personality, he made me lift my own head high.

He took another sip from his glass, then leant forward and handed it to me. It was a delicate lady's glass with frosting around the rim, the clear fluid within wafted with the spark of citrus and the punch of vodka. I didn't ask what it was and didn't care either way.

"Who are you?" His voice was softer, but no matter what tone he attempted there was always going to be brusqueness to it. "I've heard all about your reputation, Swafford. I know what it was once was. Indeed, the last time I was in California I almost had opportunity to pay you a visit. To put a bit of work your way. As things transpired, I was able to resolve it myself. But I understood from acquaintances that you were a fearsome man. You had the elegant signage to your office, but it was a pretty cage for one utterly ruthless. However…" He smiled. "You haven't been who you were for a long time, have you? So, how do you feel? Who do you think you are?"

I shook a little in my seat and nearly dropped the drink. He took the glass from me gently.

Trembling I moved forward, shaping to stand.

"Who are you?" he demanded.

"I'm Algernon Swafford," I murmured finally.

He nodded. "And what did everyone – rich man with a problem, or lowlife wracked with fears – know about Algernon Swafford?"

"That…" I stammered, the words choking sharp

and uncomfortable in my throat.

"Come on!"

"Algernon Swafford belongs to no man!" I hadn't said those words for a long while. To hear them burst forward again made me take a gasp of relief. I think, for the very first time since I fell and badly scraped both my knees when I was six years old, I had tears on my cheeks. And the incredible thing was, right then, it didn't matter to me. Let this man see me have a brief burst of womanliness. I had gone too far into disgrace to worry about maintaining appearance.

"Who is Jacob Ravens to you?" he asked.

"He's a bastard!" I seethed.

I stared at this man. I couldn't comprehend how he'd done it, but he'd opened my guts and performed surgery on me. Put my damn spine where it should be.

"Does Jacob Ravens own you?"

My tongue chewed around my mouth, my teeth ground, a self-righteous nastiness which had once been at the core of my being rose again. "No!"

"Are you his slave?"

The fury was bubbling within me, as was a sickness. There was a nagging in my guts, a sac of vomit and bile, which I had to tear apart to get those words out.

"Come on. Are you his toadie? His servant? The filth beneath his feet?"

His cool eyes on me, a familiar hardness came into my features. "No, sir, I am not."

"Good," he purred, stepping forward with a dancer's grace. His hands touched my shoulders and he pulled me to my feet. Then he embraced me. Not long ago I'd have struck a man if he attempted to touch me in such a way. Would have hit him and then beat him as he lay prostrate on the ground. In the grey of the dressing room, I let him do it (although I didn't return the embrace). At that moment it seemed so right. Strange, I felt more myself than I had in a long time, but in the tears and this sudden intimacy, I may as well have been nothing more than a young girl.

I wasn't going to hit this man, I told myself. There was no way I was going to call him a pansy. Ours was a brief acquaintance, but I already owed him a debt.

Belloc stepped back, his arms on my shoulders and his gaze filled with compassion. It was a long time since I'd seen anything kind in a pair of eyes. Lately it had only been terror or pity or darkly amused cruelty.

"Most importantly of all," Belloc's voice was barely above a whisper, "will you help me destroy Jacob Ravens and everything he stands for?"

"Yes!" I said definitely. "You have my word. I will kill him and I will enjoy it."

Algernon Swafford was truly free!

With one nod of satisfaction, Belloc reclined on the arm of the chair. His pose in an instant far more louche.

"Pleased to meet you, Algernon Swafford. The real Algernon Swafford. You are the most useful soldier I could recruit to my cause. A general, in fact. However, even with your talents and the wells of courage within you, I don't think I can ask you to walk up to Jacob and spray his brains over his expensive suit, can I?"

I was desperate to say yes. It would be a fitting revenge. My last eighteen months of torment blown away. Me putting a gun in his mouth and watching his teeth and brains splatter through the back of his head, just as they should have done the first evening we met.

But I had to shake my head sadly. As strong as I felt, I knew if I went near him there was no guarantee I could keep hold of myself. That his sheer proximity would snatch my freedom and break it apart for fun.

"Well," Belloc said, completely unperturbed. "Maybe we need to find an extra element to help you. Tell me, in all your travels with Ravens, have you ever heard the name Arthur Haberdash spoken?"

There was a blank in my mind. It was strange to think Ravens might run through his contact book in front of me. Most of the names which were mentioned in my general direction were men (and the occasional woman) he wanted to die.

"It sounds fake."

"Does it?" he replied cheerily. "I cannot imagine any gentleman going around with a moniker such as Haberdash of his own choosing. Believe me, it is real and for our purposes Mr Haberdash is the most important person in Britain."

"Why?"

"When he was a younger man, a healthier man too I understand, Haberdash was a mentor to the young Jacob. Jacob was only recently expelled from school and had the smallest amount of blood under the ends of his fingernails when he sought Haberdash out. A man who was already appreciated, through articles in fairly exclusive and obscure periodicals, as a personage steeped in darkness. Of course, there is always exaggeration and melodrama involved in these things, but it is the case that Haberdash was a deeply and darkly talented man and he taught Jacob nearly all of his skills."

"He sounds charming," I observed.

Belloc shrugged. "My understanding is his manners could do with some improvement. He isn't a confidant of Ravens now though. The two had a break, an argument. Some say a near murderous waltz. No one has been clear what this dispute concerned, but neither of them speaks of the other fondly. So, we have this man of immense power, who may have been quiet recently, but has knowledge and skills even I would struggle to imagine. What's more, he is an enemy of our enemy. And he may be able to help us.

"What I want you to do is go and see him. For various reasons I can't, but I desire you to visit with him, gain his trust. Discover if there is anything we can use to destroy Jacob Ravens once and for all."

"I can do that," I said.

"Dawn's light is on its way and so I want you to go soon. See him and when you return to London, call me." He reached across and handed me a small gold embossed card, thinner and half the length and width of a normal business card, but striking. "I want to know what it is and, more than anything else, I want to be there when Jacob is served his death. After everything I have been through, I desire to witness the expression on his face when he realises he underestimated me. That he underestimated both of us."

I nodded and tried my best not to grin with anticipated glee. "Where will I find this man?"

"Cardiff."

I knew my life would get worse before it got better, and now I had to go to Wales.

CHAPTER NINE

My father had carried a deep-seated aversion to the Welsh race which, like a lot of things about my father, he never bothered to explain. (Of course, he had no duty to explain anything to a child.) However, in my life I'd only really known one Welshman. His name was Jenkins and we served together in The War. A short, squat Neanderthal with hair so black there was no need to ever brush the coal dust out of it. He was loud, pugnacious and convinced he was a much greater wit than he actually was. I never warmed to him and the experience reaffirmed that my father's views were well worth listening to. Jenkins was the only proud Welshman I have ever met and he put me off the whole species. Whenever I've seen one – for instance, Ray Milland thirty foot tall on the cinema screen – they have always seemed so ill formed and under developed when compared to the English.

Still, with my mind clearer than it had been in eighteen months, I actually felt good about taking the train to Wales.

I actually felt good.

Time had slipped by in a fashion I neither wanted

to know or understand and I found myself in the morning. Obviously this meant I hadn't been to my hotel room and no doubt the Callicantzaros was starting to feel hunger pangs. Well, she could bloody starve for a night. Longer if everything worked out. If all turned my way, I'd get to run my own private experiment on how long one of those diabolical creatures could survive without any sustenance.

Obviously I knew my disappearance was going to be noted. Word was going to reach Mrs Ravens that not only had I vanished, but Belloc was continuing on his tour completely unharmed. It wouldn't be long until Jacob Ravens himself heard about it. Not long until he was reaching to me to try and work out what had happened. To see what he could do about it. I didn't let the thought worry me though. I felt rested and strong. There was a confidence in me. A belief I could once again take on the world.

When he had arranged its purchase was beyond me, but Belloc gave me the train ticket and instructed me to go to the Barnard bookshop at Paddington station and find a copy of this Haberdash's writings. They weren't the esoteric scribblings which had first attracted Ravens's attention, but his fiction. In the same way as his disciple, Haberdash had made money putting the things he knew to be real into seemingly made up short stories, then persuading the moribund and gloomy dregs of society who read such things to buy them.

When I first encountered Ravens, I had made the mistake of not reading any of his work. Of failing to understand the man. No doubt if I had read it, I would have dismissed it as gobbledygook, but I could at least have tried. That was my error – one of many I made with Ravens – and I was determined I shouldn't repeat it.

So I bought the one Haberdash book they had in stock, a collection of short stories. Hard backed and bound in red leather, but allowed to go dusty on the shelves. (Belloc had known exactly where it was to be found.) And as the train pulled from platform three, I settled down in my seat to read it. The problem was I couldn't make any sense of the first story. There were giants and terrible three headed serpents; there were priests who connived and murdered; and there was this heavy bosomed damsel who swung a sword as well as any man and could kill a chap by crushing him between her thighs.

My head spinning, I jumped onto the second story and there were immortals and necromancers and men who became phoenixes when exposed to the sunlight. It was nonsense, it was trash – but I tried not to lose sight of Belloc's warning: this stuff was supposedly real. In this turgid fantasy, were things this Haberdash apparently knew to be fact.

Not long ago, I'd have scoffed at the merest suggestion. My flights of fancy happened at the cinema; in real life there was only nastiness and the mundane. People may believe they were living wonderful lives, but it was all a façade. The notion of wonderfulness was a thing they reassured themselves to get through the day. Even myself, who was confident as to the quality of my life – with an enviable office and an expensive condo and a reputation which was both suave and dangerous – frequently ran into dull reality. However for me, as if the world was laughing in my face, reality suddenly turned out to be endlessly terrifying.

Ravens told me once he wrote about the space between dimensions. After all I've seen and heard, I still don't comprehend what that means – but it seemed to me this Haberdash must do the same. So I tried to prepare myself, to concentrate and make sense of all these bizarre pictures within the words. But I couldn't do it. I just kept reading the same page over and over. After all I'd seen to be true, these were merely words – they didn't connect to me as a warning or otherwise. There was no way I could make them into any kind of sense which would help me.

All I could hope was that my real life had gone to so many dark corners now, I was surely prepared for anything.

After Reading, I threw the book to the empty seat beside me. I was alone in the compartment, the pipe smoking old man who was briefly my companion had stepped off at that first stop on bandy legs. He'd looked at me briefly for a chat and I'd responded by keeping my nose in the book. Maybe he'd been a soldier as well, although if he had, I bet you it was in the Boer War. There was no way we were contemporaries.

Alone in the carriage, I peered through the grimy window. Occasionally I imagined I could glimpse a snow leopard running alongside. Incongruously brushing the trees and trampling the grass of the Thames Valley. It shouldn't have been there, yet it was. I was sure of it, the creature was following me.

Much as I could sense, behind me, a darkness brooding above London. A darkness I was going to have to re-enter soon.

I tried not to let it disturb me. I was Algernon damn

53

Swafford, after all!

CHAPTER TEN

Cardiff was a Welsh person's idea of a capital city. It was as dark, dingy and stultifyingly provincial as I could have imagined. The entire place was suffused with a kind of dreary, grey smog. Those coal mines which gave these people fuel, money and no doubt the very food they ate, seemed to have impregnated the air it was so damn dirty. But as I got off the train – into a place I had never imagined myself visiting – I realised it actually smelled of beer. The aroma of roasted hops was everywhere, in a way which might have been pleasant in small doses, but was actually quite disgusting. It gave the impression that every Welshman was solely interested in digging holes and drinking whatever swill they called alcohol – which, let's be fair, probably wasn't far from the truth.

Getting off the train, I was immediately conscious I was by far the tallest and best looking man there. For starters, I was the only one wearing a decent suit. There were others milling around in what passed for suits, but they were brown, cheap and off the rack. If you saw a man wear such a garment in Los Angeles, you would immediately direct them to the nearest homeless shelter.

My suit was from Barnaby Rhodes on Rodeo Drive, another transported Englishman, and one who could justifiably claim to have taught the West Coast of America how to dress. If Barnaby ever planned to open another store, he'd have to consider Cardiff as a location. These people needed to be educated.

Those who had made the effort of a suit – terrible though it might be – were in the minority. The others I saw at the train station were in smocks and overalls. It was noon and they were simply lurking; apparently in no hurry to get to either work or home. It seemed to me this was how they outfitted themselves to while away the hours, functionally rather than smartly or respectfully. When they didn't have coal to mine or beer to brew, they still dressed as if they were finishing a shift at a factory and couldn't wait to start the next one.

As such, when I strode down the steps from the platform onto the concourse at Cardiff station, I stood out as taller and smarter and more refined than anyone else around. Probably more than any other man in the country.

Which is undoubtedly why I was so easy to find.

I was making my way across the damp and dirty concourse, seeking a taxi rank from where I could get a ride to the address Belloc had provided, when I felt fingers tug at my arm.

My gun was under my shoulder and I was on my guard, so when I jerked around I nearly pulled this person off his feet. It didn't matter where I was, I was more than happy to punch a man in the face if the circumstance demanded it.

But before he had chance to be bounced to his arse,

he held his hands up in surrender. "Mr Swafford, please."

He was a small man who wasn't so much dressed in a chauffeur's uniform, as wrapped in it. The grey overcoat hung from his shoulders at least three sizes too big and dropped to the ground so that it covered his feet. His cap was too large so it shielded his whole forehead. Under the brim was a big pair of driving goggles and then a scarf to mask his mouth. There were Arabs in the world swathed in less cloth than this man. He was more material than anything else, it seemed.

"Mr Swafford," his voice was muffled through the scarf, but sounded high and squeaky. "Please don't punch me. I have been sent to fetch you."

"To fetch me?"

"To collect you. Mr Haberdash is eager to meet me."

As he spoke I had to lean in to hear him properly and the suspicion arose with irritation that he was putting the voice on. It wasn't natural.

"I didn't realise anyone had called ahead?" I growled at him.

Since I couldn't see his eyes or his lips, he shrugged his shoulders in exaggerated fashion. "Mr Haberdash has his ways."

I nodded. That much I could believe.

It could have been a trap. In fact it was almost certainly a trap. But a thing you learn when you've lived a life as dangerous as mine is to walk bravely into traps.

Before we could get on with it, I fixed him with my meanest glare. "Understand me though, young man." I had no idea whether this was a young man or not. He might have been older than me. The thought occurred that it could even be a lady. I kept my voice low and soft. There were lots of people around us on the concourse. Best to be polite. "I can kill you any damn time I want."

I think I heard him swallow fearfully through his layers. Or maybe I imagined it.

"Do you understand?" I asked again, carefully.

"Yes," he squeaked.

Outside the drizzle was bordering on rain. No one else seemed to mind. It's surely like the Eskimos and snow, with the Welsh having a million different words for precipitation.

I hunched my shoulders and followed the man to the car. He walked with a strange halting step: as if his legs wanted to march, but found themselves caught in an odd movement between hopping and skipping.

There were three cars parked outside the train station and I could tell instantly which one it would be. It was a beautiful black Bentley, which was polished so marvellously it gleamed in this absence of light. Between two boxy British cars, which would have resembled child's toys in Los Angeles, it was decidedly ostentatious. A car suitable for either a grand wedding or a fancy funeral. But I knew if Haberdash had received wind of my arrival through fair means or foul, then this was the car he would send.

In a city this poky, it must have made an impression. I can only imagine the reason it wasn't stolen was that it was too conspicuous to hide.

"Please. Sir," squeaked the chauffeur and opened the back door.

I leant in to feel the soft red leather of the seats and to try and get a glimpse of any potential booby traps, but all I got was luxury. With a smile to the unusual cloth covered man, I sat on the smooth seat and let him close the door.

Of course I had been chauffeur-driven before and my entire pose was of a man born to it. With a crinkle of impatience on my nose, I watched the man do his strange hopping walk around the vehicle and towards the driver's seat. He opened his door and clambered in, displaying no coordination at all. As though not fully in control of his limbs. It was a tad disconcerting.

I tensed in the seat. It would be a curious way to get rid of me: put me in the car with an incompetent driver and then wait for him to smash into a lamppost at speed. Curious, but like all deaths, not ineffective.

My hand reached for the handle, but I knew already it would be locked. Before I could do anything else, the driver had started the engine and we jerked and shuddered away from the kerb.

Lips pursed, I snarled at him: "You do know what the hell you're doing, don't you?"

Hands tight on the wheel, he turned his head to stare at me. As he did, his scarf tangled amongst the creases of his coat. Underneath wasn't a face, more a carving. A protruding chin, thick lips and cheekbones which were sharpened to an actual point. But none of it was flesh. The man was made of wood!

I gasped and watched horrified as his mouth opened and closed, exactly the same way a goddamn ventriloquist's dummy would. A lever deep within him being worked.

Without the scarf, his voice didn't sound human at all. It was too high pitched, too devoid of any accent or emotion. A phonograph record played at slightly the wrong speed.

"Oh yes," this abomination before me said. "Mr Haberdash has made sure I'm an excellent driver."

Then, to perhaps prove the point, it returned its gaze to face the road.

I lurched forward and grabbed at this thing pretending to be a man. Its shoulder was a block of wood. He was so solid I might as well have been wrestling a giant redwood. Gripping my hand around him I tried to yank him back, not caring right then if the car did leave the road and smash into a post or a bollard or even the side of a building.

My efforts had no effect. We slowed smoothly to a red light; a safe driver out for an afternoon's jaunt in his expensive automobile. I was trying to force my leg over the seat, so I could get in the front with it and force it from the wheel. Leave its wooden corpse on the pavement to scare the children.

But completely unaffected, the abomination took its right hand off the wheel and reached into its jacket. Oblivious to my frantic attempts to disrupt it, it removed a small black tube.

My back was pressed against the roof of the car and my left leg looped into the passenger seat. I was roaring, but I made the amateur's mistake of staring too long at what my opponent was doing. Ignoring my instincts, I looked direct at that black tube.

What happened next was too predictable.

Its fingers pressed a button at the top and a nozzle sprayed a peppery mixture full into my face. I coughed, feeling a rush of painful sensations I hadn't endured since The War.

My strength didn't fade instantly. Still I tried to push myself forward, screaming at this monster that I was going to pull it limb from limb and then use the carcass for firewood.

But then, in the space of a heartbeat, my anger

slipped to nothing. I was flailing at air, there was a buzzing in my ears and everything went utterly blurry.

I flopped, muscles limp, slumping to unconsciousness in the foot well of the backseat.

CHAPTER ELEVEN

There were no dreams and for that I was thankful. Given the life I led, I was always grateful when there were no dreams. After the appalling sight I'd experienced in the car, doubly so.

I burst out of unconsciousness. Only realising at the last fraction of a second that I was sitting upright and having to grab hold of the side of the chair to stop myself toppling forward. My eyes were only half-open and my other senses were swimming, but I was conscious there was someone – or something – standing above me. Instinct kicked in and I unleashed a blow. My fist connecting gratifyingly well with the head of whatever it was had been foolish enough to lurk in front of me.

My yelp echoed as I felt my knuckles bruise. There was surprise at the solid wooden knock the head gave when I hit it, then the fact that I'd sent the damn thing flying away from the body and over to the other side of the room. I had jerked myself back in the chair to stop myself toppling, but then I lurched forward – reeling with shock at the long thin wooden body, dressed in a yellow house coat, thudding to the floor at my feet.

From the other side of the little room in which I found myself, there was a sudden burst of laughter. A near hysterical screeching of amusement. It was a sound which surely couldn't emanate from a man and would only really come from a woman at the edge of hysterics.

Quickly I tried to pull myself together. My head was groggy, but I seemed to be in one piece. There were no manacles around my wrists or ankles and even my suit appeared to have retained its crease. I could feel the reassurance of the gun under my shoulder.

Concentrating on getting my heart rate settled, I peered around. The room was dingy, no more light than from a small window admitting the grey and drizzly day. I was in a parlour. One which wasn't pretty, with no wallpaper on the walls and no furniture beyond a couple of chairs. I could sense a couple of figures peering at me from the doorway, but in the room there was only me and another man. A man who was huge and screeching with laughter. The only thing he had to recommend him right then was that he did appear to be entirely human.

He was ridiculously tall. Even sitting I could tell he must have been six and a half feet at least. And he was fat, a natural portliness having been let go so extremely that every part of him – neck, chest, belly, thighs – burst with unnecessary weight. In my Metropolitan Police days, it had been my good fortune to once meet G.K. Chesterton. This man could have been his sun starved brother.

He had a shock of straw yellow hair, it grew upwards from the top of his head and spread like overgrown brambles from the sides. It also seemed to burst from his ears. The skin of his round, ugly face – his many chins wobbling at me with glee – was almost completely pale. There were two red dots at the centre of his cheeks, nothing else. When he was sleeping soundly, they'd be the only indication he wasn't already dead.

That paleness was perfectly matched by his clothes. Or the one item of clothing he appeared to have on. A white artist's smock hung from his shoulders and billowed from his girth, almost unfeasibly voluminous. It was a substantial amount of material: with the right gust of wind he would undoubtedly take off and float to the clouds. For now it draped itself over his knees, while below stuck out two pale, chunky, varicose vein ridden calves – which, substantial as they were, must struggle to support the bulk above them.

The man sat there with his ankles crossed and his hand covering his mouth to finally try and stifle his ridiculous feminine laughter.

Deliberately this time, I moved forward on my seat. Intent on standing and demonstrating who was really in charge here. But suddenly his merriment stopped and he held an index finger aloft to halt me.

"You have to be careful," he grated, and nodded towards the door. "I may have created them, they might be mine, but I can't honestly say I have full control over them. I can ask them to do things for me and most often they will, but they have become" – his pudgy hands gesticulated as he hunted for the word – "wilful. So utterly, utterly wilful. And right now, I'm afraid, they're not particularly enamoured with you."

"Why?" I asked.

He looked at the floor and amusement burbled on his lips. "Because you hurt their friend, of course!"

His voice was high, like a man who has enjoyed too much gas in a dentist's chair. However, his Welsh accent was soft. Nothing so coarse as the annoying sing-song Jenkins had inflicted on me back in The War. Obviously though, I was still thoroughly irritated by it.

"You must be Haberdash." I just about stopped myself from growling and swearing.

"Of course I am!" he screeched. "And you're Algernon Swafford. Thousands of miles from home and completely lost."

"I'm not lost."

"We'll see," he said without emotion, then perked up right from his shoulders. So many acres of flesh wobbling I was amazed I didn't feel the reverberations through the floorboards. "What do you think of my creations by the way? Impressive, aren't they? I have heard rumours that Mr Belloc – it is Monsieur Belloc who sent you here today, isn't it? – uses tailors' dummies in his illusions." He uttered the word "illusions" in a way which suggested it was the most distasteful thing he could imagine. "Well, mine go far beyond such parlour tricks. New life, Swafford, a new kind of life. As I say, impressive, no?"

I didn't respond. Merely stared at him and tried not to flit a glance to the abominations regarding me from the doorway. There were three of them, I'd guess, maybe more. I could see little flashes reflecting the light from the window. They each had china eyes in those wooden skulls of theirs – an attempt to make them more human, which simply rendered them colder and more monstrous. I was determined not to meet any of their gazes.

When I didn't answer, he took a deep breath which shuddered his torso and then kept talking. "What about dear old Jacob?" he asked. "Does he have anything similar? A marionette he can keep on a string and make dance to his tune? What do you think? Have you ever seen anything like that?" He started to laugh happily again.

I stayed still and silent, waiting for him to calm himself. My right hand on my lap, but tensed. Ready to reach for my gun the instant it was needed.

After too long, he calmed himself. There was only a limited quantity of pleasure he could derive from laughing alone.

"You were expecting me?" I observed.

"Yes, does it really surprise you? It surely can't be beyond your wit to suspect I have prior knowledge of a great many things."

"Why go to the trouble of snatching me at the station? I was coming to see you. I had your address."

He pouted a little queenly. "I doubt you had this particular address."

"Still, I'm a detective, I would have found you. Why go through all of that at the train station? Why send one of your" – I hesitated – "*creations* to grab me. It may have taken me a tad longer, but I would have got to you."

He sighed and as he did his huge smock billowed so I almost felt a draft. "Have you no sense of drama, Swafford? Really? None at all? Has your time in the West End police, or in Hollywood, not presented you with the slightest clue as to the necessity of wonderful and surprising moments in life? Please, Swafford, you are entangled in the affairs of three practitioners of the dark arts. Men who live for the showmanship of it all. A dangerous place to be, I'd imagine, for such a pigmy mind. You might struggle to make your way through."

Maybe from outside the room there was a strange titter at the insult. I did my best to ignore it. If I could get to him, there was certainly a bullet in my gun for Ravens. Maybe I'd save another for Haberdash. Belloc I was grateful to, so he could live. But I was already looking forward to the day when I watched the spilling blood of these so called practitioners.

He shifted his buttocks on his chair, striking a pose which was almost friendly and casual, pretending this was nothing more than an everyday conversation.

"I understand we have a mutual acquaintance," he said chattily.

"That's why I'm here."

He blinked once and then laughed. This time it sounded almost akin to a large bird's mating call.

"Oh, not Jacob," he said cheerfully. "I was thinking elsewhere. Do you remember Terrence Rose? Three years below you in school?"

I pondered and then shook my head. "Sorry, no."

"Really? He was quite the character and I thought, despite the age gap, he may have made more of an impression. I considered it would allow us a different connection."

"What about him?" I asked.

"Oh, it was a passing meeting. The two of us encountered each other in a backstreet brothel in Budapest after The War. He was remonstrating loudly about his bill, only he couldn't speak Hungarian and so was doing it in louder and louder English. Now, I am skilled in many languages," he said with unseemly pride. "And I was able to smooth things over, to extricate him from the premises before the owner had him beaten to a pulp. I would guess it only cost me three pounds to settle what he owed, a small amount —

particularly when Mr Rose was looking so prosperous. Well, prosperous by Hungary standards.

"Well, this man – who you might remember as a boy if you saw his photo – was a big, hulking chap. A fellow who could have played rugby football for England. Outside the establishment, this man broke into tears. Started to wail and scream in the alleyway. It was a bit embarrassing, to be honest, so I steered him to my hotel room. A homely little dive. More rats than there were rooms, but I had fun within it.

"Once in there, this Rose surprised me by pulling a gun from his jacket and sticking it to his head. Right to the side. It wasn't the biggest calibre, a .22, if I remember correctly, but it would have done the job at that range.

"What he confessed to me was fast and garbled, but I managed to get the gist of what ailed him. He said he had a wife and small child in Blighty, but he had abandoned them to go on this bacchanalian tour of Europe. He was disgusted with himself, he blubbed, but could never go back. He had gone too far into the realms of pleasure to return to a staid life. But he knew in abandoning the staid life he had let himself down badly and he couldn't take the guilt of it a second longer.

"Well, I told him it simply wouldn't do. That I would not have a fellow Britisher's suicide on my watch. I wasn't going to stand there and let him kill himself. I ordered him to hand me the gun and, do you know what? He did. He passed it trembling into my hand and" – Haberdash gave a little chuckle – "then I shot him full in the face. Four times, to make sure it was done properly. I'd always wanted to kill a man and he was the first."

I stared at him, wondering whether if I'd actually remembered this Rose, I would feel the urge for revenge. Probably not, the old school tie doesn't weigh heavily on me.

The story wasn't finished. "I screwed a virgin in his blood. A macabre little thing, fifteen years old and deeply in love with Satan. We tried a little ritual with Rose's corpse. I think it worked for me, although I'm not sure she got much pleasure from it."

For whatever reason that made him burst into laughter. I think the figures in the doorway sniggered along with him.

"I wasn't completely heartless," he continued. "I did remove his pancreas and send it to his abandoned wife and daughter so they had a memento. An item to bury in a grave with his name on, if they so wished. However, I made the fundamental error of not enclosing a note. They thought it was the boy from the butchers making a mistake – or playing a prank – and they fed the only clue they ever had about what happened to their beloved to the family dog. Oh well…"

Finally he stopped both talking and chuckling to himself, and I asked: "Why are you telling me this?"

"Because I assumed you'd remember him. That it would be a funny story about a fellow we both knew."

"I don't know him."

"Then," he said, "I think I told you so you could understand the stakes here. The kind of man I am, the kind of man Jacob is."

"I fully grasp what kind of man Ravens is."

"Yes, you've done his bidding without question for so long now. You must know all about him and all about following his orders."

I swallowed, trying to keep my blood from rising.

"I am in my own mind now."

"Are you?" he asked, his voice rising high and left eyebrow arching incredulous.

"Yes."

"And would you say the real you, the one in your own mind, is a serious man?"

"Yes, I would."

"Good." He smiled without any amusement. "You've come here today because you want to kill Jacob, haven't you?"

"I have."

"Well, you're going to have to be a serious man to deal with him. A direct man who doesn't deviate or hesitate."

His eyes narrowed, they seemed to me as dull and flat and lifeless as any of his creations.

"I am direct."

"Well, we'll see won't we?" He sneered. "Time will tell if you're the assassin we're looking for."

CHAPTER TWELVE

After the briefest pause he chuckled again (a sound I was truly starting to despise), but when he spoke it was impossible to miss the seriousness of his tone:

"The first time I met Jacob, he was little more than a jumped up scamp," Haberdash waxed nostalgic. "I can see from our brief acquaintance that you're a man who despises arrogance, aren't you? Particularly in the young. In your view, it is misplaced and unwarranted in the youthful. You also loathe femininity, don't you? Well, the young Jacob would have made your skin crawl more than I imagine the older version does. He danced around, loud and full of confidence, intending to bludgeon both men and women with his sheer exuberance. You'd have hated him. Me, on the other hand. I adored him. I am a man," he ran a hand through his hair airily, "for whom impudence has a great appeal.

"We became friends, partners after a fashion. We wrote together, made love to the same women together, performed rituals together. Spurred each other on to greater and darker experimentation. Recognising from the outset how gifted in that department we each were.

"Of course, the two of us killed together. In the darkness of the Cardiff docks, we met a merchant seaman who was so drunk he could barely stand. Drasma, his name was. Luko Drasma. Jacob had already done research and so we knew he was a right unpleasant sort. Slitting his throat wasn't the hard part then. It was the getting the body here unnoticed. It was disposing of it after we'd finished with his entrails. The corpse lay on the dining table of this very house for weeks, until the maggots had gorged themselves fat and juicy."

I leant forward and gave him my hardest gaze. "Are you trying to shock me?"

"No," he giggled. "Would you like me to?"

"Scare me then?"

The laughter died, the expression on his face turned around so it was an amused frown. "Is there really much which scares you these days, my friend? Apart from the obvious, of course."

"What do you mean by that?"

"That the same thing which scares you scares me. Jacob Ravens himself."

I continued to stare at him.

"People think I'm a forgotten man in a forgotten place. No one comes to Cardiff for power these days. Apart from a few nostalgic druids, no one seeks it in Wales either. I'm sure Jacob thinks I'm an irrelevance who can be ignored. But there is power here and, since I am virtually alone in what I do, I use it all.

"I've known about you for a long time. That Jacob had reached a certain point of prominence where he couldn't kill anyone he wanted anymore – except for reasons of purest pleasure, of course. And I know this is when he chanced upon you. A big storm trooper of a man who was brutal in a whole other way to him. That he lured you in and broke you. Smashed you apart and reassembled the pieces in a way which suited his purpose."

My jaw tightened. I didn't reply.

"And when that story reached me, it chimed all kinds of chords because there was a dark day when he broke me too." He sighed with a melancholy which in the instant seemed more him than the hysterical laughter. "I'm sure big, strong specimen that you are, you have seen violence and a half in your boots on the pavement existence. And I'm sure, in the time you have been with Jacob, you have witnessed things which you can have scarcely credited. But the thing is, in actual fact, you've seen so little.

"When he abandoned me, when he stripped all I had and determined to take on the world by himself, he left me in a whole other place. A literal, pigmy minded man such as you would barely believe it, but he abandoned me on another plane of reality. Dumped me with my soul spinning and my mind split asunder, in a land where beasts and man vie together. Where the true power lies with the old gods and the only chance I had of surviving was to become a god myself.

"I wasn't a hunter and I wasn't a warrior. So, the only means at my disposal was to become a deity. It was the sole route I had to try and make my way back. To force my will onto the strange and new world to the point where that world itself bent."

A murmur of pride crept in his voice, but there was too much sadness apparent to really chime through.

"He left me to die, but I didn't die. I re-emerged. He must have thought when I did appear from the darkness, it was as a weaker specimen. That the things which used to be second nature would now been burned away. The miracle of my survival, he no doubt concluded, would leave me emptier. He was right, of course, but in many ways he was also wrong. He no doubt thinks I'm weak, obese and of no concern to him whatsoever. That I'm far removed from his glamour and fame and the darkness he has constructed for himself. Yes, a great number of my innate gifts are gone, but when I was on my quest of survival, I learned enough to compensate. It's hard to become a god without developing a range of impressive knowledge and this knowledge has many forms. Much of it far too opaque to ever be useful in this reality, but there are other nuggets which…"

He smiled at me, but also frowned at the same time. "This is a distinctly long winded way of saying that one thing I did learn – and one thing I made sure I learned – was how I could exploit and prey on Jacob's limitations."

"Limitations?" I asked.

"Look how eager you are. Despite yourself. A born killer to your soul, aren't you?" His lips pouted. "Yes, there is something in this sordid world of ours Jacob doesn't have control of. Or at least, will stop him having full control for a short while."

What he did next was basically a conjuring trick. He may have sneered at illusionists, but was clearly not far from one himself. His hand opened and there it was in his palm. A small, round metal circle, scuffed at its outer ring but otherwise unnaturally shiny.

"This is the Croaix. In other realms it has the power of life and death over whole domains. I have seen millions of creatures fall at its command. Here, its innate force isn't nearly so dramatic, but it will still – if you bring it into the presence of Jacob – blunt his powers. He will be helpless in the face of it. Now I'm sure, with only a little time, Jacob will re-exert himself and obliterate its effect. He is that powerful. But it should present a direct man like you with a window."

"How big a window?" I demanded. "How much time will this thing offer me?"

"If I were a gambler," he mused and gazed theatrically towards the grey of the outside world, "I would say a minute or two. No more than that. But a minute will be enough time for you, won't it? A big strong man, a brute of a man. A man who knows not to hesitate or choke in these circumstances. You understand how to make the most of a chance."

I nodded. Picturing Ravens's startled and terrified face already. Relishing the thought of my sweet revenge. "It will."

He raised his hand, making to throw this strange glittering disk at me. Then paused. "All I ask is that you use a knife. Preferably serrated. I'm not going to tell you how to do your business, but – for personal reasons – I'd love to hear of a righteous individual sticking a knife in below his ribs and then turning it ever so slowly."

For the first time I grinned at him with real amusement. "I'm sure that can be arranged."

"Good. Thank you."

And then he threw it. It didn't move like metal – my eyes widening as I watched it – rather the blasted thing seemed to be floating through the air. There was no breeze I could feel in the room, but to look at it was to see it glide along on a gust of air.

Catching it wasn't difficult. All I had to do was

conquer my astonishment, reach up and pluck it from the air. It was cold on my palm, unsettling to the touch. For a moment, holding it sickened me. The sensation wracked my body that instead of me gripping it, it was gripping me. I felt a tightness around my spine, an unnerving anxiety racing through me. But then when I squeezed it tighter, determined to control it, I felt suddenly and strangely safe. In a heartbeat, I felt powerful along with it.

An unnatural lightness flooded into me, and I knew I could sit there and hold it and do nothing else for hours on end. All I would do was try to explain to myself everything I felt from it, all the waves it sent through me.

That was a trap and, feeling half-drunk as I was, I recognised it as a trap. It hurt me to do so, I knew that letting go of it would feel like a burn to the hand. But also I knew holding onto it much longer would mean I may never let it go.

Tension coursed through me, my neck muscles bulging, I managed to slip it from my palm into my trouser pocket. There was relief that the sensation didn't vanish completely. In its place I felt a confident glow, no longer an overwhelming presence.

"Now then," Haberdash gave a little chuckle, "it might be time for you to get in a little practice of violence before you confront him."

"What do you mean?" I asked. My voice a bit woozy, trying to get a grip on reality again.

"Well, I told you you'd upset my friends, didn't I? They're not very happy with you at all and they want to do something about it."

Then he gave a squeal as one of his life size ventriloquist dummies, marched through the door, its hand carved into a blade.

CHAPTER THIRTEEN

So lost was I in staring at Haberdash, in feeling the sensation of the Croaix, that the first abomination was almost on me before I had my wits fully in place.

How best to describe this inhuman thing? It was nearly six foot tall and naked, carved seemingly from a block of solid wood to resemble an athlete. Muscular shoulders, a tight waist, powerful legs and a face with china eyes and an open mouth and no other features. The fact that its eyes were so cold made its cry of rage more horrific. It screamed as it approached. A sound unlike any I'd heard before – more a letting go of air, the hiss of a snake slowed on a gramophone so the noise struck deadlier.

I don't know if it had different hands for different occasions, or whether it was built to stab, but the point of its sharpened fingers flew through the air and nearly sliced apart my skull.

My heels jerked my chair back out of its way and I toppled over with it. As I fell, I yanked the gun from under my shoulder. Fortunately it came loose at the first try, as I wasn't sure I'd get another. All I could do was fire on instinct. Before I crashed onto the floor,

I'd let off two shots – one bursting through what passed as its left eyeball and the other hitting its mouth.

There was no flesh for my slugs to pierce, but the force of the bullet sent the thing crashing off its feet. It landed with a thud which rattled the whole house. I had no idea whether it would be enough. Could bullets kill a damned thing like that?

Lying on the floor I glared at it, waiting for it to move – daring it to move.

"Well done!" called Haberdash, his voice high with excitement. "But be warned, there's always one more."

The thing which came through the door next was a mockery of a woman. Nearly six and half feet tall and wearing a flowery summer dress with an askew blonde wig. She carried a hammer and chisel and was going to use one or both to prise me apart.

My first shot did nothing, just left a big, black hole in the material of the dress, but probably went not much further than an inch through the solid bulk of wood. None of these things were going to have an actual heart which was vulnerable.

It was nearly on top of me when I fired again. Once more I managed to split apart one of these creatures' china eyes. Its body dropped with a resounding thud, lying prone on the floor. Firewood ready to go.

Swiftly I pulled myself to my feet, standing with my back to the wall.

I had two bullets left and I didn't trust either of those things not to sit bolt upright and come at me again.

"What are they?" I demanded.

Haberdash kept chuckling. "I already said, they're my toys, my creations. A man has to have a hobby after all."

I glanced at the two on the floor, they weren't moving, but it felt as if the house around us was. There was a creaking sound, from the rooms behind me and above me and below me in the basement. It was a sound the kind of which I'd never really heard. The closest I could recall was listening to the California redwoods in a heavy wind. It had the same feel: something that wasn't really alive coming horribly alive.

"How many did you make, you bastard?"

"More than enough!" he sang.

There was no time to hesitate. I strode towards the door, my gun on Haberdash the whole time. What good it would do me to shoot him, I had no idea. It would probably enrage these things, rather than intimidate them. It was more to let him know that if I was going to be torn to pieces, then he was coming with me. Though the way he chuckled suggested he wasn't bothered either way. The crazy never fear death and this man was crazier than most.

I checked the Croaix in my pocket and stepped into the corridor. Breath held in case splintered fingers fell upon me in an instant.

Ahead of me was the front door, twelve feet at most. Maybe I should have run for it, but I could feel the movement behind me – sense the hatred over my shoulders – and I couldn't stop myself from looking.

There were dozens of them. A number dressed in suits and dresses, but most naked to their lacquered skin. They were tall and short (more than one actual ventriloquist dummy size); both old and young, either brand new and varnished or faded and chipped. There were those which had limbs shaped into daggers and scythes; others missing arms and legs, but carried along on the fury of the crowd. They were marching as a solid block along the hallway towards me, trampling each other down the stairs, throwing open a hatch from the floor and clawing their way up from below. Every one of them with a snarl and a palpable desire to inflict violence.

Waving my gun helplessly I staggered on my heels. They weren't intimated by me. There were two bullets left in my gun and, even if I could refill, the most I could get off was eight shots. They'd have removed my limbs from my sockets before I managed that. My only advantage was that I was faster than them.

I turned and ran and with my heart racing. For a second I feared I'd misjudged. I focused on the door ahead and the little Yale lock, but behind me the army of monsters felt much closer. Not a threat that was going to get me in a moment or two, but one which was going to rip me apart me right that second. The gun nearly dropped from my hand, but I squeezed onto it with a gasp. It wasn't going to help me fight them, but I might need it should I feel a hand on me.

Surely not even Jacob Ravens could begrudge me killing myself in this circumstance.

All it could have been was three or four steps to the front door but in my memory it feels like minutes of fear. It was a chase which made my heart nearly explode.

However all of a sudden, the door was yanked open by my trembling hand and I slammed it behind me. I was outside. Staggering forward half a dozen paces to grab myself distance, I then turned and risked a darting glance. I was stood on a nondescript street of red bricked terrace houses, a .45 in my hand, regarding the front door I'd exited with a panting fear. It was undeniably a gate to Hell.

I expected them to burst out behind me, to drag me back in, not caring if my screams would shatter the peace.

It didn't happen.

Evidently Haberdash was happy to have his fun at home, but didn't want his skill to be too public.

And so I stood on this wet, damp Welsh street, a big man in a fancy suit with a large gun in his hand. Anyone who happened to glance through a window and see me would have thought I was reeling from a nightmare.

Which, of course, I was.

CHAPTER FOURTEEN

The walk to the train station took more than an hour and a half. It included a couple of wrong turnings, as well as an attempt to follow a set of ridiculously wrong-headed directions from a lady who looked so regal when I met her on the street she may as well have been the Queen of Cardiff. Finally, my feet aching and my toes damp, I made it there.

Part of me expected to see the black Bentley waiting. Engine purring, eager to drag me back to round off unfinished business. But they were letting me go for now. I owed Haberdash for the Croaix, but my exit didn't make me think kindly of him. Maybe though, I would buy a serrated knife out of gratitude. It seemed as good a way as any other for Ravens to meet his death.

The train I caught was the five past one to Paddington and I walked nearly the length of it before I found an empty carriage. Then I reclined in a seat and stared out the window the whole journey. How long had I been unconscious when they drugged me in the car? Was this even the same day?

I took reassurance from the snow leopard being

with me. It was my companion, making itself known as the train moved off. Only ever a glimpsed shadow behind the trees, but there the whole way. Behind me were the echoes of laughter, artificial and barely human; while ahead was darkness. That big, black cloud waiting for me. However, with the Croaix humming in my pocket, I knew I was as ready for it as I could be.

Back in London, I stepped off the train with a confident stride. I'd deliberately not placed my hand on it, but it was impossible for me to ignore the buzz of the strange medallion. So chipper was I and conscious of the simpler pleasures of the world around me, that I actually paused to help a pretty young mother off the train with her pram. She was Welsh, but I didn't hold it against her. Charmingly wishing her a happy trip to London and smiling gratefully when she wished me the same in return.

It was my awareness of the world no doubt and the fact I was feeling more myself than I had in a long while, which allowed me to spot him so easily. A large man, with an air of menace he'd obviously been cultivating.

He was broad shouldered with a perfectly bald head and acned face, but it was the eyes which did it. Narrow eyes, those of a hunter. He stood on the concourse peering directly at me. There were others gazing the same way, of course, since I was emerging from under the station noticeboards. Yet there was something different about him. He didn't have the harassed air of a man waiting for a late train. No, he was scanning the crowd hunting for a specific person and this person wasn't one who was going to wave at him when they got there. As I strode into view, he did virtually nothing to disguise I was the man he was watching for.

The realisation he was there didn't affect my stride. I walked normally, pretended I hadn't seen him and waited for him to approach. There was no tap on the shoulder, he didn't get that close. So this then wasn't an ambush. It wasn't what had happened in Cardiff. Instead, it was something else. And until I could work out what it might be, I decided to take him for a stroll.

Rather than hop on the tube, I walked into the low winter sunshine and headed on foot in the vague direction of my hotel. Through the district which had actually been my patch in the days when I was a policeman.

For me, it was a little trip through the environs of memory lane; for him, it was exercise.

Of course, things had changed immeasurably since my day. That bastard Hitler had literally let bombs off across the neighbourhood. And with Britain being your poor spinster aunt who you'd rather forget all about, there was no money to pay for her to be spruced up.

More than once, I turned a corner expecting to see a building I knew – a public house I'd had to knock the door on, or a home I'd taken tea in – and found a pile of bricks. Still, five years after The War, nothing but rubble. They hadn't managed to clear it away, let alone build anything else.

There was one whole street I used to walk down, which now seemed to be waste ground.

It was a heartening surprise then when I did see a building I remembered. A corner shop, for instance, which was trading under the same name I'd known. I recalled there had been a pretty young shop girl working there, with the widest green eyes it had ever been my pleasure to meet. I did think of popping in to see whether she was still employed, if the intervening years had been kind to her, but after not much reflection I decided I couldn't see the point. What was I going to say to her if she was there? An old lady with thick ankles. Really, what was I going to have in common with any of the civilians I knew back then?

Besides, as much as I was finding my reverie interesting, I had that fool following me. And what a bad job he was making of it. Not only had I spotted him instantly, I'm sure any passer-by would have recognised what he was doing as well. He was a lobotomised Sydney Greenstreet. There to play the villain with no subtlety whatsoever. And given he was hardly going to blend into the crowd to begin with, that was a major detriment in his current line of work.

This was either going to be a kidnapping, or harm was intended to come my way. Kidnappers tend to pride themselves on having a bit more finesse, thus it meant harm. That was fine. I was happy to take my chances against such a man.

Indeed, I had my fun with him. I took occasional streets fast, while others I ambled along – judging how close he got to me each time. Watching as he dawdled at a corner, pretending to be seriously interested in an unlit cigarette, while I stopped and paid attention to a particularly nicely painted royal blue door. It was equally funny to stroll around a corner and immediately race to the next. Hearing his running footfalls as he did all he could to keep in touch with me. I ducked into alleyways, to see what he would do if I fell from sight. Each time he gave himself away further. He was bad at his job. Terrible at it. He was useless at staying hidden and he must have realised he wasn't intimidating me.

So unworried was I by him that I let my mind

wander.

There was a street at the edge of Marylebone where a girl I knocked around with used to lodge. Really, she was the only girl in that immediate post war period who I had any kind of long term thing with. Maureen was her name and she was tall and willowy, with long blonde curls and an accent which was a close approximation to aristocratic.

Of course, in reality she was no better than she ought to have been – a Newcastle slapper to her core – so she was never marriageable material. (My parents were alive at the time, but I think I would have killed my mother with shock if I'd brought fair Maureen home.) For a young bobby on the beat, needing to amuse himself, she was entertaining enough and we had a lot of youthful fun. If I remembered rightly, she was a big fan of Chaplin. Or said she was. Whenever we went to a picture show together though, I clearly recall sitting in the back row with her and her never seeing the film at all.

There was a song she used to sing when she was in her cups. As I say, she sounded posh, but was really the daughter of a factory worker (or a gravedigger, or a fisherman. A, no doubt, salt of the earth fellow who spent every spare penny from his week's earnings getting paralytic in the nearest hostelry.) She had realised though she needed a better past if she was going to get on properly in London. Anyway, she had this song and it was about ship-hands. Probably it was a North Eastern ditty, but in her newly found received-pronunciation vowels, it sounded oddly soothing. If I went there straight after a shift, she'd sing it to me. After I'd broken a few heads, or helped a toe-rag with memory problems make a full confession, she would stroke her fingers through my hair, cradle my head on her lap and sing that tune to me.

It struck me I couldn't remember the words or the melody, yet I felt sure I'd know it if I ever heard it again. That it would give me the calmness it always did.

Maybe Belloc had tinkled a version of it under his fingers for me the other night.

The realisation came also that I had no idea what Maureen's last name was. Perhaps I'd never been sure of it. There was no way I could discover what had happened to her. Although, I wouldn't really want to if I could.

Lost in the oddly sweet remembrance, I slipped into the alley past the flat which had once been hers. Hoping perhaps that seeing it afresh from the courtyard would bring the song to mind. Would make this woman who, a long time ago had meant a great deal to me, come into clearer detail.

Maybe the imbecilic gorilla didn't realise he was following me into a complete dead end, into a shielded spot where he couldn't pretend he knew how to hide anymore. Or perhaps he'd had enough of being taken on a run-around.It didn't really matter what was going through the thing he called a mind. All that mattered is when he got within a step of me, I reacted.

CHAPTER FIFTEEN

To be fair to the worthless bastard, he wasn't a total clown. When he came near me, he made sure he had a knife in his hand. Eight inches long, solid Sheffield steel with a black hilt. With a smile, I noted it was serrated.

Maybe things were different in London where guns weren't so freely available, but in LA it was the kind of knife a low-life pimp would use. A weapon which could be deployed to keep people in line and which would be silent if it were ever needed.

This one wasn't so silent, this one didn't do him much good. When I spun around and grabbed him by the elbow, the damn thing clattered out of his grip, bouncing on the cobblestones beneath us. It was then I broke his arm with a resounding crack.

The sound echoed around the courtyard and seemed more brutal in the cold air. The man buckled, inadvertently positioning his skull so it was more at my height, then gave a sharp intake of breath. I was quite impressed with him for not yelping with pain. His watery blue eyes met mine, hurt and fury intermingling, then he swung at me with his left fist. His weaker arm.

The blow was pathetic and easy to block. Mine wasn't, and I sent a pile driver right into the centre of his soft belly. He doubled over with another gasp and I drove my knee into his nose.

Perhaps it would have actually been laugh at the top of my lungs funny if I'd been able to take a step out of myself and watch it. As it was I was too close and the adrenalin was pumping. But this large, unhealthy, bald man seemed to spontaneously attempt a backflip. His heels flew into the air, his spine twisted to an angle which made me wince, his arms waved helplessly at his sides (the broken one trailing that bit behind the rest of him) and then he came to Earth with another crack. This time right to the top of his head.

Incredibly he remained conscious, his skull clearly all bone and no brain matter. After all the exertion, he was lying prone and staring woozily at me, although his expression was groggy and his eyes were going in different directions. There was a thick line of blood dribbling from between his lips.

Maybe I should have had more compassion for him – he was clearly nearly gone already – but my fingers were already on my gun.

I hoped it would focus what was left of his mind, that he'd wake a little. Instead, to his wandering eyeballs, it was probably just more air.

"Who sent you?" I snarled.

No response. Only more dribbling.

I could have shot him then, yet – in the moment – it seemed too bloody easy. So I slipped my gun carefully into the holster. Then, I raised my foot and brought it with full force onto his slack lips.

A few seconds later I did it again.

Five of his teeth flew from his mouth, the others

which I could feel crunch apart from his gums dropped into the base of his throat – choking him. His lips were obliterated and his jaw became a mushy pulp, I didn't stop until I heard the gurgling of blood in his throat. There was no admiration of my handiwork until I was certain I'd drowned him in his own fluids.

Of course I knew this courtyard, knew how secluded it was, so I didn't expect a round of applause for my efforts.

But one came. A single set of hands slapping together enthusiastically. A feminine cry of "Bravo!"

I spun around, my gun appearing as if I was a fast draw in a John Wayne movie.

Before me was Emilia Ravens.

She was exactly as beautiful and deadly looking as she had seemed the previous morning. Particularly with the sparkle of delight in her eyes. She was wearing a black dress which clung to her so ludicrously tightly, no lady would wear it to a funeral unless planning to upstage the corpse. That choker necklace was around her neck and matching the ruby's brightness was a red pillbox hat. The only concession she seemed to be making to the cold was an obviously expensive fox-fur around her shoulders.

"Well done, Mr Swafford!" she called and I thought for a second she was going to whistle. Become a washer woman drooling over a parade of soldiers, but fortunately she remembered she was of a better class. "It's actually the case you're everything I've heard and more."

CHAPTER SIXTEEN

She drove a slick blue MG racer and she drove it fast. When I informed her where I was staying she claimed to know it, but the route she chose went right across London. Evidently she was going to keep me talking to her for as long as she wanted – damn my convenience. Almost the first thing she did when we sat together in the low, cramped front seats of the sports car (I couldn't help but notice her skirt rising a few inches to a glimpse of her stocking tops – not that such vulgar displays affected me), was cheerfully confess that she'd hired the goon to assassinate me.

"I'm sorry about the whole thing," she said breezily, her tone guilty of nothing more than swiping the last biscuit from the barrel. "One is supposed to retain a pretence and nod towards good manners, so what I'm about to tell you is a secret I haven't even confided it to my closest friends – not that I'm particularly fond of my closest friends. But the continuing existence of my husband is becoming more and more of a great irritation to me. And so the fact he had his own violent little lapdog in the same city as me was a circumstance which could – if I let it – cause me considerable worry.

"So of course, I did what any forward thinking Twentieth Century girl would do, I made arrangements. I met the dearly departed back there through a contact of a contact and paid him handsomely to get rid of you after you'd dealt with Belloc. Of course, you then managed to fool us all by spending the night at the theatre and then heading for the godforsaken wilds of Wales, but the money was obviously good for if and when you returned to London. Which of course you would. Mackerel, his name was. Or Pike, perhaps. Whatever it was had a fishy quality. Anyway, he'd deal with you and then Jacob would have no tools of destruction in this country – none I couldn't finesse out of the picture anyway – and I would be left to plot in peace."

I was spluttering before she was even halfway through. "But you're his wife!"

Even her slightly mocking titter was delightful. "Please," she drawled. "You don't believe in the 'happily ever after' nonsense, do you? And certainly not when it comes to us. I mean, you've met Jacob and I'm sure you've heard all kinds of salacious stories about me. Truly we are not the type The Brothers Grimm wrote fairy tales about. Or maybe we are, only not in the good way."

It was true, of course. The first time I'd met Jacob Ravens he was entwined with another woman – and a Latina to boot. As for Emilia Ravens, rumour had it there are Soho sluts who've been going round the block since I was in uniform who are less experienced in a bedroom than she was.

And I wasn't naive. I'd been an LA detective a long time and knew husbands betrayed wives and wives betrayed husbands. It was part of the reason why I myself had never entered into vows. But still, I didn't expect a wife to boldly say she was plotting to do her husband harm. Even if the particular husband was Ravens. It didn't seem proper at all.

Spinning the car around a corner without the use of brakes, she continued: "I tell myself there are lots of marriages like ours. I mean we have good times and bad times. Days where we're madly in lust and days where we can't stand to touch each other. I'm sure most women would confess – if really pressed on the issue – that they'd happily kill their husband if opportunity was put their way."

Once more she went too fast around a corner and this time she rather impressively made a lanky policeman leap to the pavement. Stumbling on his heels as he did.

"Oi!" he yelled after us, blowing his whistle immediately.

She ignored him, or maybe barely noticed his existence. Her shoulders gave a little shrug of delight and she shot a grin in my direction. Even with the speed, she looked so cool and beautiful behind the wheel. Utterly confident, to the extent I didn't grip the side of my seat as furiously as I should have.

"Besides," she continued, "now I feel glad my ineffective assassin didn't kill you. Actually happy the money I paid has turned out to be wasted. As, would I be imagining it, Mr Swafford, or do you seem different? More upright in the shoulders than when we first met. Carrying more of your own energy?"

I didn't answer her.

"Let's see if I can get your story straight in the head." She eyed me with a side glance, not caring what might appear in the road in front of her. "I, on Jacob's command, send you to Belloc yesterday, with the instruction to try and gather whether he means Jacob harm. If he does, you were to kill him. Belloc *most definitely* means Jacob harm and yet you didn't kill him. Instead, you spent the night with him – talking or sleeping or maybe something else…"

I grimaced at her inference. Another woman, in a different circumstance, would be counting her feet on the floor for such a slight.

"You eventually leave him and get the first train to Cardiff," she continued. "Who could you have gone to see Cardiff?"

"I think you know who I went to see."

"That old fart still going, is he?" She laughed. "Well, well, well. I've heard about him, of course, but I've never met him. Obviously he cannot mean Jacob anything but harm. Did you, Mr Enforcer, kill him?"

"No blood was spilled."

"And so you've retuned to us and you seem more confident than the zombie with the promise of violence I recently met. At The Ritz, you were clearly a bruiser who'd unthinkingly take direction. Now, I'm really not so sure. If I'd stepped in back there and instructed you to leave my man alone, to help him, take him to the nearest doctors, would you have? Would you? I don't think so. In fact, I think if I'd done that, I'd have peered down the wrong end of your gun, wouldn't I?"

The car raced straight across a junction without her glancing either way. "Have you lost a few years, Swafford? I really do believe you've dropped at least half a decade you were carrying. I think you've become more handsome."

She winked at me and I shifted a jot uncomfortably

in my seat. Flirtation had always made me uncomfortable; flirtation with a viper doubly so.

There was a minute where we drove in silence. It didn't feel quiet, at the same time she raced through the gears and swerved once to avoid the backside of a big red omnibus. Then we nearly smacked our rear end into a vegetable cart being pulled by a brown dray.

"So, let's say whatever hold my husband had over you has been snapped, what's your plan?" she asked. "What are you going to do?"

"What makes you think I have any kind of plan?"

"Come!" she tittered. "You can trust me. You think you hate Jacob, but it's nothing compared to the depth of revulsion which I have for the man. I even tried to kill *you* because you were too closely aligned. But I realise you're a charmed fellow, that you have a certain luck to you. A certain magic. That Jacob had every reason to be wary of Belloc and, possibly, he has underestimated the old fart in Cardiff at his peril. The evidence is all in you, Swafford. You have the belief all of a sudden that you can get the better of Jacob – it's there in every, confident inch of you – and whatever it is, I want part of it."

She leant slightly towards me in the seat, only half an inch or so but I was suddenly inhaling perfume as erotic as a Moroccan desert. This lady had a quality of magic herself and she knew how to use it. Her left hand left the steering wheel and she held it tantalisingly above my thigh, ready to give my muscles a squeeze should I prove to be a good boy.

"Haberdash…"

"The old fart in Cardiff," she corrected me, clearly – for whatever reason – not wanting to hear his name.

I nodded. "The man in Cardiff gave me an item."

"What did he give you?"

"It's small and round. An amulet, almost. He called it a Croaix and he said it would remove your husband's power."

Her eyes widened and came completely away from the road. "Permanently?"

"No, not permanently, but I was assured long enough for me to…"

I let my voice trail off and she nodded, before swerving the car to avoid hitting the pavement – a trick she managed one handed.

"Good God!" she exclaimed. "I had no idea such a thing existed. But now I do, I'm glad it's in your hands. Do you have it with you?"

It vibrated against my leg, not far from her stray hand, but I kept my face a perfect blank.

"Okay," she nodded. "Let's say it's within easy reach. You just have to get you and it near him."

"I'm planning to book passage on the first ship I can find. He'll realise things aren't right before I arrive, but I bet he'll choose to see me." He was more than arrogant enough for that.

"You know, Swafford," she trilled, "you might be luckier today than you can possibly imagine."

"How so?"

"Because word reached me this morning – as it always does these days, in a blunt missive – that Jacob has arrived in London."

"What?" My surprise made my voice leap high.

"Ironic, isn't it?" she said. "I pay close to four hundred pounds to have you murdered, so I can have peace from prying eyes in this miserable city. But before the assassin has got to you, I receive word that God himself has arrived." She shrugged and as she did placed the dangling hand back on the wheel. "I think it's supposed to be a gift for my birthday. Not that birthdays matter much to me now. What would be a much better gift, obviously, is your gun in my husband's mouth and you making him suck it."

I nodded, grimly, readying myself for the task ahead. "Where is he?"

"He wants me to pick a place to meet later. Shall I suggest the Addlestone Hotel? That's where you are, isn't it?"

I pondered it for a few moments. I'd already, as second nature, mapped its dark corners where I knew I wouldn't be disturbed.

"Yes, please." I told her. "Do that."

There was a change of clothes and fresh bullets in my room (though the two in the barrel would be more than enough). Plus, the serrated knife the would-be assassin had wielded was tucked carefully next to my gun. With the Croaix glowing in my pocket, they'd be all I needed. Obviously he'd know it was my hotel, but he wouldn't see me coming. He wouldn't even suspect I was capable of coming at him.

"Shall I say eight o'clock?"

"Please do."

"What about Belloc?" I asked.

"What about him?"

"He said if a misfortune was to befall your husband, he wanted to be there. He wanted to witness it himself."

She laughed loudly. "Of course he does! There are few men alive who have more reason to hate my husband than Belloc does. To be honest, he might not have the most generous thoughts towards me either, but I'm sure for this we can call a truce. Invite him along, we can all spit on the corpse together.

"Would you believe," she laughed beautifully, "when I was young I remember driving while drinking from champagne flutes? Driving fast and reckless and still barely spilling a drop. I wish I had one, I'd propose a toast. Here's to a memorable evening, Mr Swafford!"

She pulled right next to the kerb, scraping the wheels as she did. Actually it was closer to the dead man in the courtyard than my hotel, but obviously this was my cue to exit.

"All the best," she beamed at me, wondrous looking, her skin so smooth and her face perfectly symmetrical. There wasn't a painting of a devil or an angel anywhere in the world half so alluring. "Tonight, my fusty friend, you are going to make a lot of people very, very happy."

CHAPTER SEVENTEEN

However, I didn't go to my hotel room, not even to change my suit. Certainly I didn't check on the Callicantzaros. She could have starved for all I cared. If the stories about them were true (and Ravens's flunky denied they were, though there's no reason I would believe him), she would cease to exist come midnight on New Year's Eve anyway. Why bother spending time and effort to feed a creature which was essentially a deadly butterfly?

No, I made my way to the hotel, but I didn't go in. Instead, in the mounting gloom of the evening (the Welsh drizzle having followed me to civilisation) I stood outside and waited. I watched.

Like a character from a dime-store thriller, my collar was turned high, my expression was determined and there was a gun under my arm. I stood in the darkness and clutched the Croaix in my pocket. Feeling its power, revelling in it. Confidence passed into me in a glorious burst of colour, I grew into myself. I'd always considered myself unstoppable and thanks to this strange magical device, I suddenly was again.

What I was waiting for was a glimpse of Ravens

himself. Obviously, he wasn't going to stay in the same hotel I did. It would be much more his style to stay in The Ritz, along with his wife. (Or along the corridor from his wife, both with knives drawn.) This meant to keep his appointment he was going to have to arrive from elsewhere. Within a taxi which was a repurposed hearse, no doubt. I was waiting for him. Wanting to see my prey, wondering if I should spring my surprise on him early. To bring my retribution down on him and enjoy the terror on his face as I did.

I'd worn a mask for so long. I suppose, when I was in charge of my own destiny, there was my mask of civility. I always made sure to appear a pleasant and approachable chap, even to those who had paid me to eliminate a nuisance. Especially to them. I understood my own mask though. It was mine. Since I'd met Ravens, the mask I'd been forced to wear had obscured everything about me. It was black and featureless and, if it loomed out of the darkness at you, then it meant certain death. Too many people had seen my mask in the last year or so; too few had seen the real me. With Belloc's influence, with the Croaix in hand, Algernon Swafford was returning. Not the unthinking monster, but the man who belonged to no one. The man who made his own decisions as to who to kill. And I was going to make Ravens look right into my face before I murdered him and hear my voice as I gave him a final send-off.

So far, however, he hadn't appeared. I stood there, shielded in the alley across the road, for two hours. My coat buttoned tight, but the damp finding a way through. There was no sign of the bastard. No cocky stride, no smug insouciance. All I had was my slightly dingy hotel and, as eight o'clock struck, a taxi arrived and Belloc climbing into the night air. Standing there on the kerb and seeming oddly apprehensive.

His expression shouldn't have been a surprise. If Belloc could have dealt with Ravens himself, he would have done it. He wouldn't have needed me, or the man in Cardiff.

Pounding my feet three times to the pavement to get circulation flowing, I departed the alley and crossed the road to him.

Our conversation earlier had been terse. I hadn't had many coins to put into the phone-box and so was only able to get the barest details across to him before the beeps kicked in. I hadn't had time to tell him how powerful the Croaix really was.

His gaze when he met mine was steely, despite his nervousness.

"How confident are you this item will work?" he asked directly.

I kept my voice low, mumbling. "As sure as I can be."

"As sure as you can be?" he repeated and whistled a little at the sentiment. "Is that confident enough?"

"This isn't my world," I snapped, "or never was previously. All I hear now is talk of spells and other realms and random concoctions of words I would have dismissed as nonsense a couple of years ago. Obviously, I don't understand it. But you sent me to Cardiff and I retrieved an object which might do the job. Whether it's going to work, I don't know. But I'm prepared to believe it will. I'm prepared to kill the bastard." My voice became deathly calm. "You said you wanted to be there when it happened, but if you've changed your mind, tell me. I'll send you a postcard when I'm done."

His eyes widened and then he laughed. "You really are the Algernon Swafford I heard all about, aren't you? I have faith in you, my friend." He reached up and patted my shoulder. "And I'm glad I was able to reaffirm your faith in yourself."

His foot stamped to the ground, giving the impression of a Nazi officer coming to attention, but fortunately he didn't go as far as to actually salute.

Keeping my face impassive, I moved past him and climbed the three steps to the hotel double doors. Under his tan overcoat, he was wearing a charcoal grey suit, which he had badly complimented with tan loafers. It couldn't be claimed The Addlestone Hotel was the height of sartorial elegance, so his fashion faux pas didn't make him obviously stand out any more than his shortness did.

That wasn't why, in the lobby, we were as congruous as demons in a cake shop.

As we came through the doors, I saw a dozen of the endless revellers from the lounge bar had taken up squatting space in the far corner. They were all sloppy, far too relaxed. Dressed in suits but on the road to becoming the dregs of society. Anything should have gone there, but actually they made sure the two of us obviously didn't fit in. We moved with purpose. Both of us strode forward with a cold deadliness and an intent impossible to miss.

It was past time to do what we had to do.

I had hoped I'd have a few minutes – Ravens not having arrived – to determine the absolute best spot to ambush him unobtrusively. After all, I didn't want the most altruistic act I'd done in years to put me at the end of a hangman's rope.

But before we reached the reception desk, I saw her.

She was quite impossible to miss. Emilia Ravens marching towards us with a determination which matched our own. Although hers was a hundred times more eye-catching.

The soon to be widow was wearing a red dress, her hair curled and puffed up since this afternoon. A pair of magnificently expensive earrings dangling and complemented the ruby which was forever attached to her neck.

In her left hand was a long cigarette holder. The cigarette had extinguished and I wondered how many offers she'd had to relight it. Surely with her looks and the scarlet dress she wasn't going to have hidden unobtrusively.

Or maybe she intimidated as many men as she aroused.

She stopped in front of me and took a draw of non-existent smoke.

"Swafford," she kept her voice low. "And you must be, after all this time, Mr Belloc."

"Madame Ravens," he said coolly

Neither of them offered their hands. They regarded each other silently for ten ticks of the clock, malice and resentment not far below the service.

"Come on," she addressed me and turned at her hip. "It's time for you to kill my husband!"

CHAPTER EIGHTEEN

She led us across the lobby, through the heavy doors and started to ascend the staircase I had come to know so well the last few weeks.

The stairs were poorly lit and more than one guest must have turned an ankle in the shadows. But the air of privacy it gave was reminiscent of a confessional. Still Emilia Ravens kept her voice low. The three of us knew there were times when walls literally did have ears.

"He's playing one of his games," she whispered, the anxiety was unmistakable in her tones too. "He's always playing his damn games! First of all, he makes his way to this grim mess of a city without telling me. Not to surprise me. If he'd wanted to do that, he would have arrived at my suite and made himself at home. No, the point of all this is to unsettle me. Once he's here, his assistant contacts me to arrange a meeting. Fortunately the little weasel of an assistant doesn't know me and so has no way to tell how surprised his announcement made me. I casually pretended I'd been expecting Jacob all along and, in agreement with Swafford here, arranged this meeting.

"Then I got no response."

She sighed melodramatically. "It's all a game, you see? When I called the assistant again and demanded to be told why Jacob believed he could treat me this way, the assistant let slip that not only was Jacob in the country, but he was already in this very hotel. He had apparently come here to check on his little blood sucking Greek bitch, and hadn't left yet. There was briefly the runaway hope that we might get so lucky she'd feast on his entrails, but life isn't like that for Jacob. Such accidents aren't going to befall him. No, his fate needs an individual with guts to actually step forward and take the bastard down."

She turned around and her dark brown eyes met mine fully. We'd only reached the first floor, each of us moving with a slow and deliberate pace. Neither of my companions trusted each other. As grateful as I was going to be if this all worked to my advantage, I didn't really trust them either.

Besides it made me feel a tad uneasy that Ravens had been here this whole time. Rather than me waiting for him, he'd been waiting for me.

"Is he in my room?" I asked.

"Another one on the same floor. And it cost a pretty pound to get that information. Lord knows what he's been doing all afternoon."

Belloc, in his blunt Germanic went straight to the crux. "Is he expecting us, madam?"

She stopped, halfway up the next flight. I think the smile she attempted was meant to be reassuring, but it slipped to nothing in an instant. "I genuinely have no idea. Would it truly matter if he did?"

One tense breath was held between the three of us. It was the last opportunity any of us was going to have to turn around and quit the whole business. None of us took it.

"You have this object of yours?" she asked me.

"I do."

"And you're sure it's going to work?"

Belloc muttered. "I have asked him much the same."

"As far as I can be," I said, "Haber-" a raised eyebrow from her stopped my tongue. "The man in Cardiff was sure it would give us an opportunity."

My arm brushed against the knife in the shoulder holster as I moved.

"Okay," her voice dropped to a deeper level of hush. We had reached the doorway to the second floor. "If you're wrong, if *we're* wrong, then this is going to be a short and disastrous voyage into the abyss. But this is the chance we're going to have to take isn't it, gentlemen?" The slight flirtation she put into the word 'gentlemen' I could only assume came from force of habit. "Because if it works…"

She let the notion hang there and steadied herself, before smoothing the skirt of her dress and puckering her lips. I hadn't noticed it in the lobby, but her mouth was painted the same shade of red as her outfit. A couple of degrees brighter than blood.

"Here's how I think we should proceed," she whispered. "I'll go first. I don't know if Jacob is with that thing, or whether he's pumping at one of his tarts. It doesn't really matter. I'll go first and Swafford, you come with me. He's aware we've met, so it will make a kind of sense. Mr Belloc, the instant he sees you he'll realise the danger, so you stand in the shadows. Wait until Swafford does what he has to do."

Belloc nodded. "I understand. I want to be there at

the end, but I understand."

"Do you know which room he's in?" I asked.

But it was clear when Emilia Ravens opened the door that it didn't matter. Her husband was in front of us, letting himself out of the room across the corridor from mine. He was dressed casually in loose black trousers and polo neck, a man clearly not expecting to do anything special.

At first the expression on his face was mild bemusement, then there was a sort of acceptance of Mrs Ravens and I maybe being together. It only lasted a few seconds. His was far too suspicious a nature. In a heartbeat, his eyes narrowed as he regarded us. He knew there was something very wrong.

In the face of him, her chic calmness evaporated.

"Go, Swafford," she yelled, bracing herself against the door frame. "Do it!"

CHAPTER NINETEEN

I didn't hesitate, almost charging at him, the Croaix gleaming in my hand. No longer did I feel so damp or cold or old and helpless. Once more, I was the man I was supposed to be. Not the slave who half existed in a hell-scape of this bastard's making.

The effect on me was galvanising; the effect on him was instantaneous.

His smug and endlessly confident smile fell collapsed in on itself and he staggered backwards a step, mouth gaping. There was utter horror writ large over his entire face, his eyes bulging. It was so delicious to see. No longer was he the saturnine matinee idol, he was more a helpless fop.

And then, if the reaction couldn't be any more perfect, his knees went soft beneath him.

I can remember a maiden aunt of my mother's fainting at a brass band concert in Hyde Park. She said it was the emotion of the music, when everyone knew – although strictly never mentioned – it was the copious quantities of gin she consumed. Ravens almost emulated that old biddy. He collapsed downwards at his joints – the knees and the hips giving way until he lay crumpled on the floor.

Oh, it was a delight to witness.

I threw the strange amulet into my left hand and grabbed the knife with my right.

"I've been waiting for this a long time, Ravens!" I spat at him. "Now I've got you right where I want you. I'm going to do what I should have done in Monterey. Give you a damn painful death. Make you see how utterly worthless you really are. Do you think because you've mastered the devil's own skills, you're a great man? Do you believe you're a master? That you can treat me as dirt and not earn retribution?"

I took a step closer to him. Through sheer willpower, no doubt, he'd found the strength to force himself onto his knees, but he resembled a willow about to be blown to firewood in a storm. Slowly, savouring it, I pressed the blade against his throat.

"You're a jumped up bastard who learned too much wrong and unholy. You're going to rot in hell, Ravens and you deserve to be there! You deserve all the endless pain and suffering which comes your way."

Ravens' eyes bulged a little more, if that was possible, and I realised from the squeak of the hinges behind that Belloc had come through the door. He was going to be here at the end for his enemy, exactly as he wanted.

"Hurry, Swafford!" Emilia Ravens hissed.

It irritated me to have a woman tell me what to do, especially when the bastard clearly wasn't going anywhere. A minute, maybe even two, I'd been told. I had time.

And I wasn't quite finished with him yet.

"Every hour of every day I've known you, I have despised you!" I growled at him. "I've wished you dead. You made me kill so many people who had done nothing wrong, simply on your cruel whim. I love to kill, I love to hurt, but only when the person deserves it. They never did when you were picking, did they? I haven't killed anyone who deserved it for a long time. Not until now. You deserve it! And no death I have ever inflicted has come wrapped in so much pleasure."

The Croaix was literally glowing in my hand, I think it was actually humming a tune. Smiling, I bent my shoulders and pierced the knife through the material of his jumper. An inch below the ribs, as Haberdash requested.

Emilia Ravens and Belloc both appeared at my shoulder. The confidence from the amulet was contagious. They wanted to be there for the messy bit at the end, to see the innards spill out of him.

We all held our breath waiting for his scream. Waiting for the blood to spray as I twisted the weapon.

An utter silence of dark foreboding filled the corridor. All of us, including the man on his knees, anticipating the denouement.

But my hand wouldn't move any further.

No!

I couldn't press it home, not even when I tried to throw all my weight forward, my arm wouldn't move. With every ounce of my body I wanted it to, but my hand was paralysed.

No! Goddamn it, no!

Ravens raised his jaw and his gaze met mine. There was far more force in his eyes than there should have been. A greater, unnatural power.

Either the Croaix had stopped working, or he'd exaggerated his weakness in the first place.

Emilia Ravens was the first to realise, she gasped and then stifled a scream.

There was sweat on my brow as I tried one final time to lunge. To do what I was surely put here to do – the righteous thing. But instead, I was a statue with his dark and malevolent eyes boring into me.

Everything seemed to slow.

Belloc turned, soundlessly I think, and tried to run. He wasn't going to make it far. The entire world had dropped to quarter speed, every action was long and painfully drawn.

My right hand yanked the knife away from Ravens's side. I may as well have tried to threaten him with a colourful child's comic book for all the good it had done. Desperately I tried to resist, wanting to reach for my gun and blast with the two bullets. However, I wasn't in control of my actions.

Ravens had me. He straightened himself up from the floor, no longer suggesting a scintilla of weakness.

The knife dropped to the floor. Involuntarily, my arm rose upwards.

Emilia Ravens stood beside me, while Belloc was only halfway through his turn.

I raised my hand and then hit it down on the bedroom door next to mine. Forcing the handle open.

At the same moment, I think I screamed.

CHAPTER TWENTY

The Callicantzaros burst from the opened bedroom door. No longer a disgusting little secret, her hunger making her reckless.

She had elongated even further since I last saw her. Her head and shoulders were stretched so that both seemed to end at blunt points. Her stomach and waist were narrow and emaciated, and her whole being cried with insatiable craving. The blood curdling shriek she gave was triumphant at having found food. Her mouth opened wider than any wolf's, her fangs bared and her claws waved – deadly weapons scything through the air.

I jumped backwards – time having jerked again to normal speed – and knocked Emilia Ravens staggering.

Neither of us was the target. Ravens had as much control over this creature as he did over me.

Belloc barely had time to utter a gargled scream before its fangs sank into his neck. He dropped to the carpet and she followed him, pinning him there, enveloping his torso. Her entire disgusting, grey and naked body shuddering and spasming in ecstasy as she gulped his warm blood. His viscera splattered onto the walls, spread across the carpet – a burst dam of red.

I don't know if he tried to push out with his own power, to use his own magic, but he didn't get a chance. There were no grand final words, no spell he could mutter to save himself. His jugular was severed and the abomination of a creature chewed through the bones of his neck, grinding her fangs on the muscle.

Behind me, I think I heard Emilia Ravens's cry with shock and alarm. Did she ask her husband for mercy? I couldn't really follow her words, but I know she wasn't talking to me anymore.

My head was spinning and all I could focus on was the grisly sight in front of me. It was too late for any goddamn mercy.

Ravens had risen to his feet. Without looking at him I knew that to be the case. He wasn't pretending to be weak any longer. I was physically the bigger man, but he loomed above me.

Paralysed as I was, the impulse did not come from within me. It should have done. Certainly it should have been what a man of action did to save Belloc – a chap he had reason to be a little grateful to. Or, at least, to avenge his death. But the familiar weakness had settled onto me again. When the gun was pulled from my holster, it wasn't strictly my choice.

It was Ravens's.

Belloc convulsed in front of me. They were death throes, but from the brief glance I got of the man's eyes, it didn't look like he'd reached the point beyond pain.

And obviously, while Belloc was suffering, Ravens wasn't going to let me do anything.

The blood splattered onto my shoes and Belloc's arm waved frantically. Maybe he'd have managed a final bellow of agony if his throat was intact.

In a single instant, he went completely still. It was then my finger pulled the trigger.

Both bullets flew good and true into the spine of Callicantzaros. If she had such a thing as a heart then I hit it true. My shots left neat little holes and puffs of grey powder where her own blood should have been.

She slumped on top of the pianist. A creature who was much more a wild and dangerous animal than she was human.

In cinema and plays, there are crucifixes and stakes. Obviously that kind of thing didn't matter with a Greek vampire. A .45 would do it. I stared at the two dead bodies and the blood on the floor and smelled the excrement where Belloc had evacuated his bowels, as well as the unearthly stink which came from that creature of nightmares. Even though it was a tiny movement, I could sense Emilia Ravens trembling at my side. And gradually – only gradually – strange really for how loud the sound was and how much the joy of the moment consumed him, I heard Jacob Ravens laughing and laughing and laughing.

CHAPTER TWENTY-ONE

I didn't look at Ravens, instead I listened to him pull himself together with a giddy gasp of air. If there was someone he felt friendlier to nearby, he'd probably have slapped them cheerfully on the back. He subsided from hysterics to the kind of cold calmness which comes over men when they've just had two people killed. Or one person and a monster which used to be a human.

When he spoke, I knew his voice was going to contain a revolting, triumphant purr.

"Every day I could feel him plotting." He was peering at Belloc, giving him a eulogy of sorts. "He wanted to come near me, but he never got close enough for me to strike out first and do him harm. I had to lure him from under his rock, make him think he could win. And what better tool to use than a guileless idiot like you, Swafford? I think you might be even more useful when you think you're acting for yourself."

That familiar dread pressed heavy on me, the one I'd lived with for endless months. The helpless sense I was seemingly destined to endure for the rest of my days. My confidence and sense of self evaporated. Deep within a voice yelled in rebellion, but I knew I couldn't listen to it.

He stepped forward and, proving I was irredeemably helpless, took the Croaix from my hand.

"Eight seconds," he said. "That's about how long it truly affected me. I'm sure the man in Cardiff told you to be quick, but obviously he didn't hammer home the need for utter urgency. If you were the strong, silent type I night have been worried. But I knew you'd want to have your say, to give your righteous condemnation, and that your say would stretch. I knew you wouldn't disappoint."

With a little effeminate moue, he leaned in and pressed his lips to my cheek. My hands were numb and helpless, so I couldn't wipe it off, let alone push him from me.

I don't know how he did it, but he crushed the metal amulet in the centre of his palm. It seemed to dissolve to dust.

Emilia Ravens was cowering against the wall, perhaps imagining she could escape, or her husband would forget she was there. Instead, with a little pirouette, he stepped back and yanked her hand tight into his. She winced, maybe shrapnel of the Croaix was embedded in his palm.

Or perhaps she'd promised herself she would never be touched by him again.

Even as he moved, his eyes never left me.

"Despite everything, I knew I could trust you, Swafford. That your predictability meant you could be relied on. Of course you hate me. Why wouldn't you? I knew your hatred would power you on. You'd take anything the man in Cardiff threw at you. Bring his prize possession to me and I'd learn for myself how worthless it really was. But more, I knew I could rely on your consuming contempt to march my main enemy right to my door.

"As for you, my dear." He shot a glare to her with a snap which sounded like a shark bite. "I can't quite decide whether I feel betrayed, or whether I expected this all along. Possibly it's a point in the middle. Maybe I'll laugh it off, or maybe I'll punish you – we can decide in the bedroom later."

A transformation took her. Her shoulders straightened and the fear was replaced by a kind of sultriness. Whatever was going to happen, he wasn't going to kill her right then and she responded to the realisation. She became, in a matter of moments, the kind of blowsy damsel who can turn a man's head – even those of us who've no interest in Mediterranean looking sluts.

Their eyes locked, contempt and hunger mixed together. A disturbing and depraved sensuality.

"I hate you," she whispered. "I will always hate you."

He grinned. "And one day you will kill me, won't you?"

"I will." She meant it, even as her words were breathless with cheap melodrama. "I promise you with everything in the blackened husk I call a heart!"

Forgetting I was there, they leant in and kissed each other. A slobbering, full mouthed kiss which should have been kept in the bedroom. A photogenic couple grinding together in a way which felt as cruel as it did lustful. They lingered at it, before she pulled herself free and spat a mouthful of phlegm in his face.

He wiped it off with a laugh.

The two of them kept holding each other's hands, their fingers twisting together, as Ravens gave a satisfied glance at Belloc's decapitated body and the horrible, stinking corpse of that creature.

Finally he regarded me, wearing his most charming smile – pretending we were friends.

"I have booked every room on this floor, so there's no chance of this" – his nose crinkled, the whole thing now apparently distasteful to him – "being discovered soon. Swafford, you need to make sure the corridor, at least, is clear when the maid arrives. Of course, she or the manager is going to have the shock of their dull little existences when they finally pull away the 'Do Not Disturb' sign on whichever room you dump the bodies in, but we'll all be long gone by then. Tidy this place, pack your bag and return to Los Angeles as fast as you can. I think you'll be safer there."

"What about me?" asked his wife. "Where will I be safest?"

"Oh, with me," he said breezily. "Although it's also the place where you'll be in the most danger."

She gave a shrug and for a second I thought she was going to laugh. It would have been a dark sound if she had, it was hard to miss the malevolence smouldering from her.

Our eyes met for a second. Hers were full of rage, regret and fury. We'd failed and all she could do was clutch his hand and play at being some kind of wife.

"Goodbye, Mr Swafford," she uttered without a trace of emotion. "I'm sure I'll see you again."

The two of them stretched their legs and almost made a dance move over the blood; casually, as if for them it wasn't really there. Or was nothing more than a muddy puddle in a Hollywood musical. With the

119

same exaggerated grace, they moved towards the door and once there Ravens grinned at me.

"Do your normal good job, man. That's why I keep you around after all. You do what I want and you do it so well."

Then they were gone. And I was left with the dead bodies and a voice within which wanted to break free and roar to whatever might exist in the heavens.

CHAPTER TWENTY-TWO

I slumped against the wall once the door was closed. My breath held, the stench of defeat on every inch of me.

Essentially he'd done exactly the same as I had to the silly journalist. Lured them to this floor with a promise and let the inhuman demon loose on them.

Maybe he and I weren't too far apart then.

No, I couldn't allow myself to believe that. He had done what he had done because he was evil personified; I had done what I had done because I was contaminated by him. I'd never have embroiled myself with such a hellish creature of my own volition.

Even if Hell was obviously my final destination too.

A furious voice called from my centre, swearing it would get revenge. It had been quiet for too long, but now I knew I'd never lose it.

Briefly I'd felt like myself – the Algernon Swafford who belongs to no man. It had been passing, perhaps it had all been illusory, but it was there. My sense of self had returned and I couldn't lose the memory of how good it was. How right. Nothing in Ravens's dark power was going to take that from me.

One day I was going to be there for the death of the bastard, Jacob Ravens. I swore it to myself. I didn't know when it would happen, much as I couldn't really conceive how. But if I wasn't going to kill him with my own hands, then I'd make sure I witnessed it.

In the immediate, however, I had blood and bodies to clean away. I let the blackness of my mask reattach itself.

A Note from the author

If you enjoyed The Hellbound Detective, then do check out the other entries in The Ghostly Shadows series. The other terrifying instalments: Death at the Seaside, Certain Danger and Won't You Come Save Me and Call of the Mandrake are now available. Each is ostensibly a standalone, but if you read them all you'll start to recognise the connections…

In addition, if you have read and enjoyed this novella, would you please take the time to leave a short review of it on Amazon?

Reviews are the lifeblood of an indie author. They make the difference between scrabbling along and actually making a living out of our writing. So, if you're able to find the time to leave your thoughts on The Hellbound Detective – or any of my other Ghostly Shadows tales, long or short – then I would be tremendously grateful.

Kind regards,

FRJ.

OTHER BOOKS IN THE GHOSTLY SHADOWS SERIES

All available in paperback.

DEATH AT THE SEASIDE

Nothing was going to ruin Castle's holiday, except the mocking laughter of the dead…

Larry Castle was anticipating a lovely few days at the seaside. Basking in the sunshine, canoodling with his mistress and playing the big man visiting town. However, a chance encounter leaves his confidence reeling.

There's a possibility that someone knows his darkest secret. The thing that made him, but which could equally break him. No matter what, Castle is going to have to deal with this problem. Otherwise it could cost him everything.

This weekend Castle is going to confront the ghosts of his past, but some ghosts are more real than others…

Death at the Seaside – a gripping new supernatural thriller which could chill on even the most uncomfortably hot day.

The first in the Ghostly Shadows series.

CERTAIN DANGER

What are those voices from the past? And why are they screaming at her?

It all started when she witnessed a car crash. A brutal smash which left a gorgeous young couple dead. But for Alice, it reawakened strange memories of childhood: a sinister old house, a dead boy in the woods and an other-worldly power lurking forever in the darkness.

Desperate to make sense of the bizarre pictures in her mind, Alice's enquires lead her to a hidden away clinic in the Surrey Hills. Within those walls though, are the terrifying secrets she's been running from her whole life.

Now, for Alice, the truth could not only break apart her sanity, it could destroy the whole world…

Certain Danger – A brand new British horror tale perfect for all fans of James Herbert, Clive Barker, Iain Rob Wright and Hammer/Amicus films of the 1970s.

The second in the Ghostly Shadows series.

WON'T YOU COME SAVE ME

The actress might be dead, but her voice keeps singing to him…

Something about that murdered woman got to the detective. She was a missing person he was tracing – a young starlet – but by the time he found her, she was a bloated corpse on a dockside. One moonless night she'd been beaten, strangled and dumped in the Thames.

Her gangster boyfriend thinks he's got away with murder, but the detective is coming for him. The need for revenge burning at his soul. He might look like an average man, but there's a new force within him – one that craves bloody vengeance…

Every night her song gets louder in his ears, but what will happen when its power is truly unleashed?

Won't You Come Save Me – A brand new British horror tale perfect for all fans of James Herbert, Clive Barker, Iain Rob Wright and Dennis Wheatley.

The third in the Ghostly Shadows series.

CALL OF THE MANDRAKE

What terrible secrets are the town's women hiding?

Beddnic, on the South Wales coast, has shut itself off from the outside world. Days after a number of its men were reported missing, the road in was closed and all communications ceased. No strangers are welcome there anymore.

Now, two agents – Ludo and Mick – are venturing across the water, anxious to know what's going on and desperate to help. And no amount of threats or horrors will make them turn back. The awful curse which has befallen this town is about to be revealed, and the dead shall walk…

But in this cruel place by the sea, will these two men really be able to help?

Call of the Mandrake – A brand-new British horror tale perfect for all fans of Stephen King, H.P. Lovecraft, James Herbert and the adventures of Sherlock Holmes.

The fourth in the Ghostly Shadows series.

ALSO BY F.R. JAMESON
THE SCREEN SIREN NOIR SERIES

All available in paperback.

DIANA CHRISTMAS

**He's been threatened, beaten and broken –
but still he doesn't regret meeting the actress
who disappeared…**

Michael, a young film journalist, is sent to
interview the reclusive movie star Diana Christmas.
Twenty years prior, the red-headed starlet suddenly
abandoned her career, leaving her fans puzzled and
shocked.

Their attraction is instant. Between the sheets,
Diana tells him of the blackmail and betrayal which
ruined her. And how – even now – she's being
tormented.

Emboldened, Michael sets out on a mission to
track down a compromising roll of film – unaware
that around the next corner lurks deadly peril.

**Can Michael save Diana from her past? Or will
the secrets which crushed her life destroy them
both?**

*Diana Christmas: Blackmail, Death and a British Film
Star – a new thriller of desire and betrayal from F.R. Jameson.*

The first in the Screen Siren Noir series.

EDEN ST. MICHEL

Avenging her secret could put a noose around both their necks…

Joe might be a stuntman, but still he'd never expect to end up in bed with a genuine movie star. However, that's what happens the night he meets the ultra-glamorous, Eden St. Michel. Swiftly they're the talk of the town. Their passion fast, intense and dangerous.

But Eden has scars from her past, both mental and physical. Joe needs to be her hero, although retribution won't be easy. One misstep could mean the end of their careers and – maybe – their lives.

After a sudden moment of violence, Joe finds himself in deadly trouble. He may have the love of a good woman, yet it's leading him to the gallows.

But what if the only way to save Eden is to make that ultimate sacrifice?

Eden St. Michel: Scandal, Death and a British Film Star – a new tale of film stars, gangsters and death from F.R. Jameson.

The second book in the 'Screen Siren Noir' series.

ALICE RACKHAM

Theirs is an affair destined to end in murder!

Thomas had never met a woman like Alice Rackham. A film-star: sophisticated and uninhibited. Not only is their passion intense, but she could help this impoverished young actor with his own career. Surely it doesn't really matter that she has danger written all over her…

As he isn't the only one smitten with Alice: her ex-lover skulks ceaselessly outside her home and keeps a former policeman on retainer. A giant of a man who would relish making both their lives torture.

With Thomas rattled, Alice suggests a relaxing trip to an English country house. But trouble isn't just going to follow them out there, it's about to turn deadly.

Can Thomas save Alice from her past? Or will it destroy them both?

Alice Rackham: Obsession, Death and a British Film Star - a new thriller of passion, jealousy and suspense from F.R. Jameson.

The third novel in the Screen Siren Noir series.

ABOUT THE AUTHOR

F.R. Jameson was born in Wales, but now lives with his wife and daughter in London. He writes thrillers; sometimes of the supernatural variety, and sometimes historical, set around the British film industry.

His debut novel, The Wannabes, which contains both horror and British actresses is available for free now from his blog, which you can find at - https://frjameson.com/

You can also find him on Facebook, and follow him on Twitter, Instagram and Pinterest: @frjameson.

Printed in Great Britain
by Amazon